BOOKS BY

REYNOLDS PRICE

LOVE AND WORK

REYNOLDS PRICE

LOVE AND WORK

NEW YORK

ATHENEUM

1968

FOR

WILLIAM PRICE

AND

PIA

AND

MARIE ELIZABETH

Ihr Gatten, die ihr liebend euch in Armen liegt,

ihr seid die Brücke, überm Abgrund ausgespannt,

auf der die Toten wiederum ins Leben gehn!

Geheiliget sei eurer Liebe Werk!

HOFMANNSTHAL, *Die Frau Ohne Schatten,* I

LOVE AND
WORK

O N E

THE phone's first ring pierced his study door, a klaxon vs. cheap birch veneer. Twelve years' conditioning—that phones announce disaster—jerked him from the desk and three steps toward answering before he remembered. He was not to be disturbed, was here but working, could his wife take a message? Apparently not—four rings, five, and no sound of Jane moving. No doubt she was deep in some life-or-death work of her own. Let it die; he would not go. But he could not return to his own waiting work. He stood between desk and door, hands clenched, jaws grating, while each ring screwed deeper into his absurd command, absurd resolve—general, tycoon, migrained duchess. Urgent business. Refuse all calls. But calls were calls for help. That had been his belief since twelve years before—the call in the night, the rush to his father, the sight of that death. The deaths of friends—already at his age, thirty-four, he had lost four friends little older than he; all announced by phone.

Still no sound from Jane and the rings went on. He would stand his ground, give her Hell when it died. (If the news was urgent, they would soon try again.)

Then last night's dream flushed downward through him, a corrosive sludge, the proximate cause of this spasm of work—cleanly dressed, he had waited in a hotel lobby. Enormous space, all but empty of guests. A few ladies milled but no one entered. The friends he expected were long overdue—thirty, forty minutes. Time enough for disaster. He sat tautly, tensely, refusing to pace; yet he could not recall the faces he awaited or, now, their names. Then the doors slung round. Two policemen entered and behind them, straggling, his friends bathed in blood, clothes torn, wounds gaping. He knew their faces, rushed to them at once—the three best men from his short-story class and the friend who taught it with him. But they did not stop, explained as they moved—a wreck, the car crushed and sunk in a rocky ravine. Then they reached solid doors, the policemen stopped him, his friends vanished silently. Their blood dried quickly on the cool marble floor—only sign that they still lived, had hope; that this was not dream but a day in life, with sequel and duties. The hotel became a hospital then; and he roamed its corridors, searching faces, peering through doors half-open on pain or protracted boredom. He could not ask, still recalling no names; but when he had wandered in circles for an hour and shook with panic, he saw a young girl—a student nurse. "Help me," he said and she stopped, unsmiling. "I am looking for four friends. They are badly hurt."—"Their names?" she said.— "Don't laugh," he said, "I cannot remember." She did not laugh so in gratitude he tried to picture each in words and gestures—his friend and three students as they had been till now, whole, unhurt. At the end, she seemed to understand, attested the success of his artistry. She led him to a phone and said "Wait by this," then disappeared. A long silent wait, the phone rang once. He answered; a voice said, "Thank God, where are you?"—the slightly frail voice of his most gifted student.—"Here in the hospital, looking for you. Are you all right?"—"All but my left arm and back. How are the others?"—"The others? But you were with them . . ."—"We were separated." Now panic was terror. Now they all were divided, all gravely hurt but him. And his memory was dissolving; names still would not form.

He had waked then, furred with dread, dim light in the room—six by the clock—had lain on by Jane for a sleepless hour, then risen quietly at seven (Saturday, Jane's one chance to sleep). He had made his own breakfast, heard the news at low-volume, the dream all the while pressing heavier. A few times before—spread years apart—he had had such dreams, not blatant nightmares but subtle and secret subversions of his calm, work, love; threats of prophecy. A whole day seemed lost already—fine day. Out the windows May leaves—not yet quite full—rocked in sun, the weight of light. He had meant to plant shrubs, a fence of climbing roses. Now probably—he read it like a sentence—he would moon about the house, unable to read, no need to write; a crippled dog, powerless to mend.

So he had suddenly phoned Ted's house—the colleague in his dream—for mocking reassurance. No answer. Seven-thirty. He had told himself that— Saturday, of course—Ted was launched early on a book-buying trip (Ted spent countless hours scouring Salvation Army stores for books which he resold at minute profits.) Anyhow Ted was gone. He could hardly wake Jane, steal her precious rest, to say, "I've had a bad dream. Hold my hand."

6

He had phoned Cal, the student (a measure of his dread—students phoned you; you did not hunt them). Long ring at Cal's apartment, then a sleepy girl's voice. God, seven-thirty; he'd dragged some girl from Cal's bed, clearly. No turning back. He asked for Cal. Long wait. Then Cal's voice rusty with sleep. "Cal, it's Thomas Eborn"—what else to say? "I dreamt you were in a terrible wreck"? A bad moment's silence, then rescue by Cal—"I've been trying to get you, sir, all week. You may have forgot our deadline is Monday." He had forgot—his promise to write a piece for Cal, fiftieth anniversary of the college magazine which Cal now edited—but he seized it gladly, lied, "That's why I'm calling. Sorry to wake you and your lovely guest but we oldsters rise early. What I need to know is, how long do you want it?"—"Any length," Cal had said, "we're subsidized—a novel if you like." Eborn laughed, "Calm down. Five pages, you're lucky; but I'll have them by Monday." Cal had thanked him heavily, returned to his girl; and Eborn had been saved—the sanity of one more day secured, and with Jane undisturbed, unsolicited.

In gratitude, he had fallen on the task—not a story or poem but an essay that had formed in his eight years of teaching, more nearly a sermon. They would read it as that—any reader under thirty—a square old irrelevant gust of wind; still he would write it. Square but true. And would write it this morning as prompt thank-offering for the dream disproved, charm against its return or delayed explosion. He had left a note by the sink for Jane—*I am in forced labor on an overdue job. Take all calls—protect me, love!—and I'll see you for lunch*. Then had shut himself in, worked slowly but

unwastefully, mind tense and focused through the hour
more of silence, then Jane's quiet waking, her padding
through bath and breakfast, more silence (she would be
in the yard now, reading in sun).

But the ringing phone—

Feet pounded up the back stairs, across the
kitchen. Jane answered, in time. He could hear soft
noises of a conversation but not the words. He crept to
his door, strained to hear through wood.

"Mr. Eborn is busy now, operator. Could he call
you at noon?"

A long-distance call, personal to him. Who from?
He was tempted to rush out and take it.

But suddenly Jane was talking louder, the caller
agreeing to talk with her—"Oh Mrs. Eborn, Tom's
behind on a deadline, that's all. Is it urgent?" Jane shut
the kitchen door at that point and the rest was brief
mumbling, then Jane again descending to the yard
and her book.

So after a few seconds' wondering—was his mother
ill or broke? neither: Jane would have called him—he
returned to his desk.

The photograph there, pushed almost off by the
morning's pages, seemed further license—stronger than
his dream of destruction on friends—for a sacrificial
lunge into work. He pulled the frame nearer. Then,
though he could feel its high brassy smell in the pads of
his fingers, he studied the picture. His parents stood on
a crude plank bridge. The sky behind them was bleak,
trees bare—November, December 1928. The year '28
was inscribed on the margin in his father's hand; and
indeed his mother's long left hand proved the year no

later—no wedding ring yet; they would marry soon, deeper into winter, January. Yet they wear no more than their Sunday suits (his black, hers tan or gray perhaps); no overcoats, scarves, hats, boots or gloves. His mother's shoes are baby-doll slippers. Yet the day is clearly cold—the air, the light. They are unprotected. They do not feel cold. They lounge, unshuddering, loose in their clothes; stock-still for the camera. Or perhaps they do not care. They smile, very slightly, at their cameraman—a friend?—though his father's eyes smile more fully inward—his goal in sight, his five years' courtship now promised reward. His mother's deepest smiling is expressed in her stance—she cants herself, confident, against his father's shoulder, down his whole left side. *They must care, must quickly protect themselves. Take shelter, in time.* They will not—did not, perhaps by then could not. Life had devoured them, struggling, but vainly. His father clawed down twelve years before by cancer of the lung; his mother now at sixty transporting in her skull a carotid aneurysm the size of a full grape, ripening to burst. What might have saved them? might yet save her?—not from pain or death but boredom, futility, a life whose final emotion is puzzlement? Especially her these twelve lonely years—seven years all but solitary since he, her one child, had left and married.

His unfinished essay—this morning's work—was his first gathered try at a usable answer, the weight of his own life pressing to yield what was not new but needed—by himself, Jane, his parents, every student he'd taught, nine men in ten. He sat now, checked the house again for silence, drew his parents slightly forward from falling, and read through his first pages, softly aloud.

There may be no reason why a man should work, provided he lives in a society which charitably supports its unemployed. The only abstract reason for working may in fact be that a God exists who created man and set man to work to glorify His creation. (The second chapter of Genesis says that God made Adam "and put him in the garden to till it and keep it.") If a man does not acknowledge such a God—and his own duties to God—then perhaps he is a fool to work. Let him sleep till noon seven days a week, leave the house only to cash his welfare checks, buy his beer and return to watch television all afternoon, half the night, surrounded by his loud and growing family.

Yet—to speak of myself—even if I did not acknowledge God, even if I were adequately supported by the state, I am sure that I would work. And my first, simplest reason for working would be one universally expressed in proverbs—that "The devil finds work for idle hands." But my next reason would be that one expressed in the motto which Hitler inscribed across the one-way gates into his death camps: Arbeit Macht Frei—Work Makes Free. *Few if any men freed themselves from Dachau or Belsen or Auschwitz by the work required of them there. But the truth of the motto survives that hideous distortion. Work frees a man. Frees him from what, though?*

First, from want—physical want, hunger, cold, disease. But I have suggested a society which would supply these wants. Exactly so.

In such a society I would work to be free of others. Free from prolonged economic obligation to the state, which is self-diminishing (and a man's obligations to his state increase paradoxically and terrifyingly as that state becomes increasingly impersonal, unreachable). But at least as necessary, free through the exercise of my proud and growing skill from other human beings, free even from those people I love, especially them.

This will require explanation. I do not mean that I would wish to be—or would ever become—free of the duties and debts of love toward my kin, partners, friends. What I mean is that only through my own early discovery of, cultivation of, absorption in some work—building houses, teaching school, laying roads, writing novels—could I free myself from the crippling emotional dependence upon other human beings which infects and afflicts any man who has nothing in his life upon which he can rely, nothing more permanent than other people. A craft, a skill may—given good health—last a man all his life; very few friends, wives, sons, daughters will prove as enduring. Age, disease, death—and worst, disloyalty—exist and will in time win all that we love. The hardest shield for ourselves will be our work, if we have troubled to discover and master and commit ourselves to some absorbing and yielding work.

But our selves also exist and are as frail, vulnerable as any other person we may have loved. Yet it is our selves which will remain true to us longest of all. All our weaknesses—our vanity, greed, dishonesty, cruelty, fickleness—will accompany us closely to our graves. What shield is there then against our own loyal flaws?

*What may free us from ourselves, our final enemy?—
work, perhaps only work, the daily commitment to a
task which will demand from us full and strenuous
exercise of our strongest selves; our comprehending,
foreseeing, order-creating minds, our miraculously com-
plex physical competence.*

*So work frees a man. Yet I have only spoken
negatively, denyingly of the things work frees us from.
The difficult but necessary question remains—what
things can a man's work free him for?—*

He stopped then, hearing Jane's footsteps
again—back-stairs, kitchen, hall, the climb to his study,
a pause outside but no knock, no word. He did not call,
so her aim diverted to the nearby toilet; and he read on,
though silently now (Jane's nearness would make him
feel painfully visible, bathed in his own light, Narcissus
at the pool).

*—I will—can only—answer for myself, by attempt-
ing to explain briefly but truthfully my discovery of my
own work, its nature and function in my life, perhaps
in the life of the world.*

*I was the son of parents who, like most Americans
at the time of the Great Depression, suffered profound
humiliations—economic and, thus, emotional—which
were inevitably filtered through their screening love to
me, their first child, born in black winter. Yet though
I was faced in my early years not with actual poverty
but certainly with the threat of poverty and though
my father (who had only finished high school) hoped
that I would want to study medicine, I have no memory*

of ever wishing to be anything but an artist. First, a
painter; then a musician—

Again Jane stood outside his door—why else but
for him? She was hardly studying pictures on the wall.
He could not read or begin to revise—that far, she
succeeded—but he held himself entirely still. He would
not call to her. He had asked her help—to protect his
work—but his work was what in the world she most
feared, secretly hated, having none of her own (a job,
yes—design at the college press), no child, only him,
and he divided by his various works of which she was
one and not the largest—his writing; his teaching; his
friends and students; the remaining ties, tough as gris-
tle, to his mother. With every moment Jane hung-fire
outside, his own stillness swelled in intensity till his
mouth and throat were awash with loathing, till his
shut eyes transmitted loathing enough to penetrate
doors, throw her back on herself.

But she stepped forward, knocked. "Tom? Pardon
me please."

He did not say "Yes" or invite her in but stood
without a sound, walked slowly to the door and opened
on her face. It did not work—her smile, her apologetic
shrug, her total appearance intent on subduing him.
His stance and expression were unforgiving.

So she said, "Listen, Tom. I know you are busy"
(*busy* not *working*) "but I'm worried a little."

"Only a little? Then why stop me?—I let you
sleep."

She splotched, quick, red—her cheeks and throat.

"We're swapping are we?—Jane's sleep for Tom's precious solitude? Well, Jane breaks the pact—your mother, Tom."

He did not admit he had heard the call.

"That was her on the phone awhile ago." She pointed to the kitchen.

He nodded. "Good. I hope she was well."

Jane waited a moment—"So do I"—then laughed, at her husband's frost, her own little fear which she'd come to state. "No, I came, Tom, because she seemed—odd, somehow."

"What did she want?"

"You of course. The call was *personal* to you. But when I told the operator you were busy, your mother said she'd speak to me—only to ask me why you were busy. I didn't know but I said I'd stop you if she really wanted. She thought that over and finally said 'No.' Then she thought awhile longer—so long I thought we were disconnected—so I said 'Are you there?' And she said, 'Oh I'm *here*. Tell Tom to phone me when he's free. I'll tell him something.' I asked again if I could take a message—I tried to be pleasant, asked how she was—but she only wanted you and she said again 'I'll tell him something.' Tom, she may be worse. Her voice was so fine. She seemed much farther than thirty miles."

He still blocked his door, still had not smiled; but he no longer saw Jane.

She said, "Am I silly? I couldn't read again so I came to tell you."

"Thank you," he said. "I'll phone her at lunch."

He took a step backward to close his door.

Jane stiffened, said "Right—she's yours," turned and left.

She was his, at last, all but totally. And he no longer needed or wanted her. Half-blind and sentenced to a bleeding death (but stoutening daily), she knew that now as she'd known his needs and desires from the start, had laughed at his child's lust, then rushed to kiss him, give him in recompense only little less than his total craving—knew and accepted with exhausted grace (an occasional joke on his monthly visit as she'd straighten his collar or smooth his hair—"Love is blind, Tom, at last!") that his life had by-passed her or broken at last from her circular field, turned now in new orbits round other poles. His marriage, his work.

This morning's work had died in the gap. As he skimmed it again, it seemed dead from the start not merely balked, not merely square wind (high-toned, elementary, humorless) but the privatest, most local of truths; meaningless to anyone less desperate than he or desperate in other ways, other hags in the saddle—anyone born after 1940, anyone with parents other than his, other eyes and hands. And worse, not even private truth but smoke-screen, fog, with not even the fake but imposing dignity of justification—his own life defended. Turbid concealment—as was all his work. Concealment of what? A hole in the heart.

He rummaged for his checkbook, flipped through his stubs. Five weeks since the last check to his mother. She was calling for money. Now he'd forced her to that, proud as she was—and broke and thrifty. ("There's one good thing about blindness, Tom. You can't see dirty cuffs or runs in your hose.") He wrote out her check (one hundred dollars), added a brief note (he'd explain when he phoned), sealed the envelope, addressed it. Sent *Special Delivery* by nine tonight, it would reach her tomorrow.

But his unfinished essay—when he looked now to that—and beyond in the room, the first fifty pages of his second novel, a copy in pigskin of his first thin novel (a gift from his editor), the picture of Jane before he had known her (a girl by a pond in a short white dress), his parents young on their autumn bridge, bare as the trees to a life of winters—he was chin-deep in ashes that pressed round him warmly, nudged his lower lip. More would sift down with each thought, each word.

He rose, walked quickly to the bedroom phone, placed a call to his mother. Four rings, five—he slammed it down. (She still always answered by the second ring, slowed as she was.) Half-past-ten. Where the Hell had she gone, in what?—twenty minutes. To Ida Nolan's, he remembered—of course; his mother's Massachusetts-Irish-Catholic neighbor with whom she spent most mornings watching TV—game shows, quiz shows—then a full lunch together. He reached to phone her there, then realized they could hardly talk (Ida's TV ran top-volume day and night). He would drive over now to see her, alone; take her out to lunch—amends and penance. He touched his face. First he must shave.

*　　*　　*

Bare to the waist in his own bathroom, he grinned in the mirror at his own simplicity. The mere decision to dress and go had lifted a weight, sweetened his mouth, even let him dismiss with a painless glance his mother's genetic triumph on his face, a face she had made (and continued to make) with no visible help from his firm ample father—a jaw already (just-post-*Christusjahr*) surrendered to the downward slide of flesh, a shrill chin made for slicing not butting, rhapsodical brown eyes, fine wavy brown hair—"a Rumanian-Jewish palmcourt violist made from lowchurch Scottish yeomen!" He also dismissed his work-essay—fake or not, he could check that later, either scuttle or finish it. But now he was free and focused for his shave. He had had a college teacher fifteen years before who was fully bearded (curly white silk, and in the fifties when beards were scarce as Communists) and who always explained to his first class each year that his beard was logical. At age twenty-one he had calculated—fifteen minutes a day to shave, eighteen thousand days in fifty more years. Nearly two hundred *days* to be spent scraping beard! It had made a heavy impression on Eborn who spent the next six months scratching a beard, then surrendered and shaved it but resolved on the spot to use that time. How? Reciting verse. He believed in memorizing, was a member of the last memorizing generation, had thousands of school-lines by heart at eighteen (Emerson, Longfellow, Eugene Field, John McCrae, Joyce Kilmer), then in college had added hundreds more of firmer worth. And he tended his repertoire each morning while shaving.

Wordsworth, this morning—*Tintern Abbey*, the poem he had tried all week to teach his sophomores. It had failed (the poem or he) for all the groups—the safe solid girls (future homemakers), the few whiffy hippies (vaguely sweet, against their will), and the future accountants (merely filling requirements). Wordsworth in the tropics was problem enough (he had faced that once on a forced hike through desert) but Wordsworth in prosperous America—and not only with the young but with his younger colleagues. Lines like

> *. . . Nature never did betray*
> *The heart that loved her . . .*

would get at most a sneer; at least, a shrug. ("But what he means by *love*," Eborn thought, "they miss entirely, having wrecked the word.") So much the worse for prosperous America, sick with the failure built into its dream (that men are equal, can be equally good); barnacled already, past scraping, with deceit; sinking slowly from the sheer weight of hot air but savagely swelling, a wallowing balloon.

He had said aloud, perfectly, three-fourths of the poem when he heard Jane pass, enter the bedroom. The poem submerged but did not stop—he rolled it on silently inside his head. But Jane did not speak so at his favorite lines, he said again aloud William's prayer for his sister—

> *. . . Therefore let the moon*
> *Shine on thee in thy solitary walk;*
> *And let the misty mountain-winds be free*
> *To blow against thee: and, in after years,*
> *When these wild ecstasies shall be matured*
> *Into a sober pleasure; when thy mind*

Shall be a mansion for all lovely forms,
Thy memory be as a dwelling-place
For all sweet sounds and harmonies; oh! then,
If solitude, or fear, or pain, or grief,
Should be thy portion, with what healing thoughts
Of tender joy wilt thou remember me,
And these my exhortations! . . .

He had told his class—half the prayer was heard.
The moon had shone, Dorothy gone mad at sixty,
William's silent agonized companion the rest of his life
and beyond till her death at eighty-five, five years after
him. (He had smiled at the end of the solemn conceit,
then ended with—no, the moon was not guilty. It was
Dorothy's fault. She drove herself mad. Your mind is
your own, give or take a rare chemical imbalance.)

He reached the end and Jane was gone—or leaving. He heard her car in the drive. Gone for groceries,
miffed. Another fence to mend. Well, later. He had the
sudden thought—as he rubbed on cologne—that he
might have seen her for the final time. What if she died
or was killed in his absence? What would his final
memory be, his final speech to her?

The sight of his smooth face, red now and tightened, canceled his fear or replaced it with an instant
fully-formed absurd theory—that the Romantic movement was a function of beardlessness. The beardless
man must spend part of each day in contemplation of
his own mirrored face. Two centuries of enforced daily
narcissism (beards vanished in Europe, when?—
mid-seventeenth century) and you begin to enjoy the
sight. Hence the Egotistical Sublime—Goethe, Words-

worth, Coleridge, Byron, Shelley and Keats. All beardless as babes. Was the notion new to him? He searched
his memory. Surely it was. If his work-essay failed, he
could write this up. Aware that his mood of quick
elation stood on silly sand, he dressed, took the check,
left Jane a note, trotted down to his car and started for
home.

It still seemed home, from miles away—the safe
place, the goal (no, the *end*) of all wanderings. He had
driven these thirty miles perhaps a thousand times in
the past sixteen years, beginning as a college freshman
himself, home each weekend as the nearest refuge from
roaring dorms, sour cafeterias. The road then had been
almost country road—two narrow lanes laid through
round pine hills, a house or a gas station every few
miles (country gas stations, no pennants or beacons).
Now, though still three-fourths black woods, there were
knots of clutter along the widened lanes, literal cancers
(proliferation of unneeded cells)—four gas stations,
each with plastic pennants, at one lonely crossroads; a
paper-walled motel never filled; a new 1930s-roadhouse
("The Sugar Shack") with black-curtained windows
and at most five cars on a Saturday night. Yet clear or
cluttered, and though he now mostly drove it in duty, a
knowledge had always come upon him, at about halfway, that forces stronger than his own guilty will had
taken control and were reeling him in—not flapping
and gasping but willing and soothed, *won* not *caught*.
It came upon him now. More than willing, he yielded;
raced in.

*   *   *

The house crouched in heavy shrubs and trees—
"squatty," his mother had always called it though it
was the only two-story house in the safely middle-class
neighborhood. Red-brick, square as a child's play-block,
oppressed by a brooding black mansard roof, it was far
larger now than his mother's solitary life required. A
three-room apartment would have been the greatest
plenty, for her bounded present. He had tried to tell
her that three years before and had almost convinced
her—"So much less to clean, Mother; no roof to leak;
no furnace to stall." But her blindness had begun and
he'd dropped the plan, never mentioning why, though
they both understood—that she needed every inch of
these ten-rooms-and-basement to store her past, her
lifetime's hoarding (every paper, picture, bolt) and to
plan her blindness and swelling death in the midst of
what still guaranteed her dignity, her proofs of a life.
He had often thought with dread of the house as a
ship—top-heavy barge groaning with debris—and her at
its heart as its only power; a ship which he must scuttle
at her death, ten years from now or any moment.

But today, with the sun, he noticed only that the
canvas porch-awning had split with rot. One repair he
need not make—take it down for good; let the buyers
worry, when it came their time. He stopped beside his
mother's small car (she still drove in daylight, to visit
friends), walked quickly to the front door through grass
that needed mowing, turned his key in the lock and
found he had locked not opened it. A counter turn; he
thrust his head in, called "Mother" once to the unlit
hall—no answer. Right. She had walked down to
Ida's.

Ida's was two houses down—low clapboard with black wrought-iron laced in every angle. New Orleans Creole Irish Catholic. He paused on the stoop to hear the TV that generally poured through bolted windows. Silence now. And the screen door opened when he tried the handle—Ida double-locked every door to halt rapists. He rang the bell. Within, a dog barked—Ida's asthmatic poodle—but no sounds of walking. He rang again—another bark, then deeper quiet. He checked his watch—eleven-forty. Surely they had not gone out for lunch. His mother's car was in sight, at home; and Ida's surely garaged, moved only for Mass. He rang once more—silence even from the dog. Then he walked slowly back to his mother's house (inexplicably abandoned, however briefly, it seemed for the first time to be beginning a slow change, reduction, into *house* not *home*).

He sat on the front steps awhile, absorbing sun; mildly puzzled by the absence. Well, he at least was here and could use the time, not scour the neighborhood hunting his mother. She would be here soon, would first see his car and would then find him working. In his old room. He had meant for years to weed his bookshelves there—keep a few pieces for nostalgia (a Hardy-Boy or so, his high school yearbooks); donate the rest to a Salvation Army.

His room was now, at last, hers. After his father's death and his own departure, his mother had taken a fall-and-winter roomer—a boy a year from the local college; and the room she had chosen to rent had been hers. Hers and his father's—the marriage room, double bed and all. The reason, she'd said, was it had its own bath and was off to itself at the end of the hall. So it was. Of the two vacant bedrooms, she moved into his—"It's got the washbasin and it's nearer the phone. You're here so seldom, you can have the front room. It's light, for your work. Tom, you don't mind, do you?" She had asked his permission after the fact, the house was hers, and he *was* seldom there; but he had minded, deeply, and still minded now with the roomers long gone—and for layers of reasons that settled in his head, a dense mat composed of eviction and encounter, longing and repugnance.

She had altered nothing, only added her dresser and a wallpapered nightstand that held her reading. The rest remained as he'd carefully made it—a lonely erotic pious artistic adolescent's lair (grotto, cave, with a Yale-locked door). The walls, though pitted by re-moved picture-nails, were still deep plum-red trimmed with gray. The bookcase matched and the screen round the basin. One picture she'd added where he'd taken one down—his father at thirty, face retouched to baby-smoothness; only the wide, propped weariness of his eyes to hint (beneath fake highlights) that his life was half-over; well more than half in terms of the weight and pressure of time. Otherwise, the decorations were Eborn's—a dark wood cross with an oddly nailed Jesus (more splayed than hung; a body exploding), photographs of Vivien Leigh and Ingrid Bergman, a portrait by Eborn of Flagstad's Isolde (furious perpen-dicular profile—no break from hairline to end of nose—as she flings her curse, more enduring than her love, like a wave at Tristan), a tennis racket, a long fox horn (neither used more than twice). The bed was unchanged—high narrow walnut scene of his raging puberty; fits of pleasure, fits of guilty prayer. No, not unchanged. She had taken that also; slept in it each night (or used it as her base for insomniac wanderings—to the kitchen, the TV, occasionally the yard).

It was unmade now—sheets swagging to the floor, pillow pounded to a ball, a faint sour odor hanging chest-high (her permanent odor, always crouched in his memory). Eborn stood in the doorway a moment, all but left. Then he took firm hold, stepped in and made the bed—or threw the sheets up, not looking at them, and smoothed the pillow. (Even in college he could never work with the bed unmade and had often wondered why—his native neatness, gift from his father, or some feared threat, some invitation?)

To test his calm, he sat on the bed. He had not touched it for more than ten years; but the no-nonsense firmness of the thin felt mattress was familiar at once, bracingly Spartan. Strengthened, he leaned to her flowered nightstand, to check her reading. He was touched increasingly as her blindness descended by the fact of her trying, as in homage to his trade, to read herself to sleep each night. What he'd normally have found—with her copy of his novel—would have been a *Reader's Digest, Your Health, The Upper Room* and occasionally an issue of *Sexology* ("Many people who don't play baseball, Tom, *watch* baseball games"). What lay there now, atop the old stack, was a small red-leather appointments diary, 1955, and a browning envelope with green one-cent stamps, addressed in his father's hand to her maiden name, postmarked 1928. They were both new to him.

He thumbed the diary first, from back to front. All blank till he came to February. There the space for each day—four narrow lines—was filled with his mother's headlong hand. February '55—his father's death. Her record of that, from day to day, in different inks. As though she had seen in the first small sign, the sprawled hideous rapid death—

Sun. Jan 23—Todd shoveled snow but got awfully tired. He doesn't feel well.

Mon. Jan 24—Todd went to Dr. today with a red throat and aching legs. Spot on his lung. Dr. Langston said it was pneumonia.

Fri. Jan 28—Can hardly walk legs hurt so badly.

Mon. Jan 31—Dr. wants Todd in hospital for checkup. No room available today.

Tues. Feb 1—Not responding to drugs. Spot still on lung.

Wed. Feb 2—Hospital calls so off we go.

Thurs. Feb 3—Very upset. X-rays etc. Small room.

Fri. Feb 4—Got a nicer room today. Todd seems happier.

Sat. Feb 5—No reports. Still making tests. Todd not so nervous.

Sun. Feb 6—My birthday. Todd gives me red roses.

Mon. Feb 7—No reports. Todd nervous. Seems resigned tho.

Tues. Feb 8—Drs. say they will do a broncoscopy tomorrow. Todd upset.

Wed. Feb 9—Today was terrible. Todd nearly strangled. I feel so sorry for him and am so anxious.

Thurs. Feb 10—Waiting for report.

Fri. Feb 11—Still waiting. They have ruled out T.B. Which doesn't help.

Sat. Feb 12—Dr. Langston tells me today that it's cancer. No one will ever know what this has done to me.

Sun. Feb 13—Todd comes home for three hours today. Between 2 pm and 5 pm. Lies on sofa talking to us. He fully realizes it's his last time home. Brave and sweet.

Mon. Feb 14—Drs. tell Todd today and advise an operation. He agrees.

Tues. Feb 15—Everyone is holding up for each other. Todd tells us everything he wants done.

Wed. Feb 16—5½ hours on operating table. 8 pints of blood. Drs. give him up and send for Tom and me to come to recovery room. He gasps for us to leave. Does not want us to see him so terrible.

Thurs. Feb 17—In critical condition but knows us all.

Fri. Feb 18—Restless thru the night. Tom stays by his side. He wants him.

Sat. Feb 19—Tracheotomy. He looks so pitiful and cannot talk. No hopes.

Sun. Feb 20—Ida and I stayed last night for Tom to get some sleep. Todd so restless till we get Tom back at 6 am. He looks at Tom and smiles and never seems to know anything from then on. No one will ever know

*what it did for me when I saw him breathe his last at
8:21 pm.*

Eborn shut the diary, torn by opposites—
admiration for the skill with which his mother had
stripped each day of that month to its bone, each slick
white vertebra revealed in its purpose (he had kept no
record, then or since, himself; but her daily ten words
sucked the whole tide back to flood him now). And her
clear foresight—her move from past-tense to present-
tense after the second day; the smell of a fate striding
down her life, which she must face *now*. But her
threadbare comments—"brave and sweet" on his last
day home! (they had spent those three hours in chok-
ing silence, avoiding his father stretched shoeless and
pale on the gray flowered sofa) and "No one will ever
know what it did for me when I saw him breathe his
last." Did for *her*? It had not *been* for her. He had not
been hers. She had not *seen* the last breath.

But Eborn also felt shame at eavesdropping here;
and he laid the diary back carefully in place, meaning
to forego the letter as penance. Yet it seemed, at once,
his—despite the address to his mother's maiden name.
The handwriting did it—the slow slightly feminine
script of his father which, even then, in his early twen-
ties was set for good. Every word he would write for the
next thirty years, through crushing blows, would be
mirror of this—all his letters to Tom.

Eborn listened a moment for silence in the
house—he was still alone. He took the letter, smelled
its strong must, then opened the one crisp page and
read—

Dearest Girl,

Have only read your letter once this morning but am going to answer now and get it off on No. 11 for you.

Dear, you have taken my letter wrong. Why did you say I had rather go to Amburn than come to see you? I don't see how you said it—as worried and as worried as I have been since your illness. Please try to get home Sunday why can't you? This is something we have got to talk over.

But before then even, drop the Alec business. Get it out of your system and love me all you can. Will you finally believe me when I say I love you all I can, all there is possible? Will you think of me as the true lover I really am and not what I appear to be? For God only knows how much I do love you. I know you love me all you can, and I know I am always the one in fault, but it is because I am so foolish over you and can't bear to think of you caring for another even for old time sake.

Please dear, love me and tell everybody you are mine and I am yours. I am so worried, so dissatisfied. Can't you hurry and come back to me and fill the place that is so vacant? Can't we ever understand that you are mine, I am yours? Lets try, dear. Lets do all we can to make each other know.

With a million kisses for my dear,
Todd.

Error. The fatal error of their lives (his parents), fatal error of Western Man!—"that you are mine and I am yours." No one was anyone else's, ever. Even Jane knew that—*knew* if not *understood*. His mother should have known it as clearly as he. What had her whole life been but a school to teach her that? Why had she dragged out these ancient lies now to block her path, when debris enough lay between her and death?— "brave and sweet," "you are mine, I am yours"? Yet despite his anger, his hands were gentle, all but cherished the heavy brittle paper, thumbed the script like fine engraving.

A noise downstairs. The front door opened, a silent pause, steps on the hall tile. His mother, home. He first felt shame and fear—caught again. "But the room is still mine." Quickly but carefully he replaced the letter, stood, smoothed her bed, walked loudly to the stairs— "Mother, I'm here."

No answer, no sound. "—I'm sorting through my books, or was just beginning."

Someone said "Tom"—not his mother—then was silent again, though he heard steps cross the living-room rug and enter the den.

He went to meet it.

Ida Nolan—marooned in the midst of his mother's den alone, her round face blotched and inflated from tears. Yet Eborn's first thought was not "Why tears?" but "How odd to see Ida outside her own house. She can still stand and walk!" (High blood-pressure and television had hobbled her firmly as a Chinese empress, her only move being Mass twice a week).

She tried to speak again—his name, he supposed—but instead blew a momentary bubble on her lips. She extended a hand (still clutching her car-keys), but he did not take it.

He stood two steps away. He could not move. "Mother?" he said.

Ida managed a sound—"Gaah"—and nodded rapidly.

He still did not move—she'd retracted her hand—but he said "Sit down" and pointed to the large red armchair, his father's.

Ida looked, shook her head; looked all around her, then took a little cheap wicker chair in a corner.

So Eborn took his father's chair and said "Tell me now."

Ida swallowed and could speak. "She is not in pain. I don't think she hurt for more than five seconds. And she'd been so well, right through yesterday. This morning she came down to me as usual—for our programs, you know, and our diet lunch! Not two hours ago. We talked a little, then our programs came on and, with them, I wasn't watching her and didn't hear a thing till she said once '*Oh*.' I knew she was speaking of pain not the program so I turned to see. She was touching her forehead, *pressing* with her thumb. Then she went slack as cloth and I rushed over to her. She did not know a thing, though her eyes were open. Somehow I got her stretched out on the floor and took her hand to say I'd call the doctor. But she gripped my hand and would not let me go. Her eyes were open and I said, 'Lou, can you hear me?' She never answered that—"

"Is she still alive?"

"She was when I left the emergency room, ten minutes ago. I had followed the ambulance but when I saw her in doctors' hands, I came to call you, back here in peace. Thank God, you knew."

He thought that out, didn't bother to correct her. Then he stood to go.

Ida struggled up. "Do you want me with you?"

"I'm all right," he said and walked through the living room toward the door, Ida sobbing again two steps behind. In the dark entrance hall, he remembered to thank her and promise her the news.

"Shall I call Jane?" she said.

"Thank you, no," he said.

"Tom, she'd want to know. Lou would want her to know—"

"She's out now," he said, "buying groceries." Then he recalled his largest question. "Ida, what did Mother have to tell me—did she say? She tried to phone me this morning. I was busy."

Again Ida shook her silent head. One more thing she did not know.

"She said to Jane, 'Tell Tom to phone me soon. I'll tell him something.' Tell me what, I wonder?"

"—That she loved you, I guess. What else did she know?"

He thought he was moving for the door, his car. He was reeling, in revulsion, one backward step before he recovered (and blamed Ida's sopped smile).

But Ida came to him, heaved herself onto tiptoe, kissed him on the jaw.

Then he went out, trotting.

Half the way there, he thought of Ida saying "Thank God, you knew." His dream of course—

approximate knowledge, parallel, metaphor. Destruction on his friends, sent on them by him however deep asleep. And beyond destruction—separation, free lives for all, himself free at last, room to turn. In answer to the dream, he had tried to work (not in vain perhaps—the essay might yet stand, strengthen in his absence); but in answer to this?—his mother's bleeding brain; sent on her; *wished* on her by him for years, in pity, impatience, embarrassment? What would answer this final abandonment?—his whole past gone? He must wait to know.

But he found her at once, contradicting his dream—found her room, at least. Though she'd only arrived half an hour before, entirely unconscious, she was already listed at the information desk. Room 321. He went there slowly on a quiet elevator accompanied only by a silent Negro boy age ten, one eye as milky as a marble—trachoma. Eborn's own eyes crouched an instant—infection—then resigned, looked ahead as the doors slid open straight onto the room, the doctor emerging.

Eborn remembered him painfully from two years before—his mother's operation—and went to him now with unsmiling recognition.

The doctor spoke first. "You must have flown."

"I was here already—on my way, I mean. I knew she was low."

"Was she?—since when? I hadn't seen her since well before Christmas."

Eborn paused a moment. "To tell the truth, she had seemed very calm, quite content and active. I was worried though."

"Now you know you were right. You'd have been right to worry these whole two years."

"Thank you, I have. Is she dead?" Eborn said.

"Not yet. The artery's blown, of course. Spinal pressure's sky-high."

"No hope, I'm sure?"

"Just *hope* there's no hope. Hope she dies today."

Eborn nodded obedience. "I hope that then."

The doctor touched him with one brute hand—no extra charge, a human after all. "Good, I'm having her sent to Intensive Care. You can go in now. There's a nurse in there." He thumbed behind him to the shut door and left.

There were two nurses, struggling in the dim light above her, their backs to him as he entered quietly. They seemed to be stretching her left arm—what therapy? The sound of the door softly closing shocked them both. They wheeled on him, staring. The young one, red-haired, dropped his mother's arm which bobbled, a stiff spring, beside the bed. Her senior—dwarfish, gray-haired, loose-jowled—said "Are you family?"

"Her son," he said.

"You can take those then—her valuables." She pointed to the table—keys, watch, twenty dollars (not broke, at least). "And there are her clothes"—blue dress, rubber girdle, white underwear flung over a chair. She took his mother's arm again—the wrist, then the hand—and the younger nurse followed. "We can't get her ring off. We're working on that. Know the combination?"

He took a short first step into the room, watching only the hand. "Can't you leave her that till she's dead at least?"

"Sir, don't look on the black side. This is routine. It's a safety policy. She won't need these."

The younger nurse had taken up a large round jar, their last resort. She unscrewed the lid and gouged with one finger a lump of vaseline.

Eborn watched—from six feet—as she greased his mother's finger, thin ring and all. The finger shone in the overhead light, slick and opal; and the older nurse began again tugging.

He strode in on them, not speaking but firmly shouldering them back.

They yielded mutely.

He took the hand—warm and soft as ever and its color unchanged, as though news had not yet descended that far—and suddenly calm, without revulsion or fear or grief, he turned the ring once, slowly drew it off. Dull platinum band, four diamond chips, holes for four more (lost and not replaced). Her wedding ring. His.

He smiled at that, freely as if alone (showed teeth, chuffed breath)—they were folding her clothes—and looked to the pillow, her upward face. The features—entirely superfluous now, mere integument, rind—only screened from sight the pouring blood. He thought of another time beside her—two years before, the failed attempt to repair her artery. He had been led into Recovery Room past rows of dying or rallying forms, to the bed where she lay still three-fourths asleep in a helmet of bandage (footballer, cyclist) that covered the shaved sliced scalp, sawed skull. The nurse escorting him had shaken her roughly—the cheerful roughness of those who know all the body can bear—"Wake up, Mrs. Eborn. Your son is here." He had winced, said, "Don't. Let her rest while she can." But his mother had heard, swum slowly up, looked and asked with great effort, dry lips, furred tongue, "Tom, when are they going to operate?"—"They have," he had said. "They have. It's *over*." She had taken his lie, sunk back to sleep, maybe soothed of terror. All that exquisite brutal effort—saws and chisels—for one hopeless look at an artery ballooning at the optic synapse, then a sickened replacing of the lid—to wait.

The nurses had finished their bustling, stood ready. Eborn said to himself, "Let it be over *now*. Ended at last." But his lips touched the ring.

That was twelve-thirty and, the ring safe with Eborn, the nurses pushed his mother, bed and all, out the door. "Where now?" he said to the younger nurse.

She whispered, as though his mother might wake or perhaps to show herself kinder than the other. "Fourth Floor West—Intensive Care."

It seemed the title of a Russian novel—the life of a woman devoted to others. Turgenev, Chekhov. *Intensive Care. Intense*, maybe better. "Do I follow?" he said.

"No," the older nurse said. "No visitors there."

"There's a lounge right beside it though," the other said and smiled.

Eborn knew he was hungry. His small early breakfast, having fueled him this far, abruptly vanished. Head and stomach ached. So he walked behind the bed to the elevator, saw them roll his mother on and rise out of sight. Then he pressed the Down button, waited thirty seconds and took the same car (that quickly abandoned—she was rushing now). On the ground floor he went to a small canteen, ate a tasteless sandwich made last night by machine, drank a warm box of milk and (blinding his vision to the slack shapes around him—not a smile in the room) said over and over to himself a vow which was really a plea, "Everyone else that I've ever valued, past and future, must die *suddenly* when his turn arrives, no illness, no wait. Just a baffled instant, then a black pitch forward. Jane and myself most of all, boots on. And entirely alone—no one watching or touching till our corpses have cooled and composed themselves."

Then he went up again, to Fourth Floor West, intending to sit in the lounge awhile till the doctor appeared or there was news or he could see clearly what his own course must be. But he saw an empty phone booth and went towards that, to notify Jane. His coin was poised to drop when he felt *No*, strongly. His reason to himself was—sparing Jane, waiting till death or indefinite vigil were a fact she could face. But he knew, beneath that, that his reason was savage—he must have this alone, as his mother would have wished it; must make her death as she'd made his birth, alone except for a few nameless hands.

Intensive Care had wide swinging doors, padded with leather, and a plaque at the side—*No Admission Without Doctor's Written Permission: Ring For Infor-*

mation. Eborn understood, for the second time, the passion of doctors and nurses for secrecy (shut doors, rude half-explanations, refusal even to divulge blood-pressure)—they would tell themselves that it simplified their work, cleared their paths of clutter; but, truer, they craved single combat, ordeal. Themselves and death, in a ring alone—or death the foregone victor; they the witness, menaced but spared, and endured alone.

He thought of the moment of his father's death. He had sat all day by the unconscious body, helping the nurse bathe, catherize it; whispering to his mother who was in and out. Then at 8:15 (the windows dark) they had been alone, his father and he—his mother in the hall with friends; nurse gone for medicine. He had pulled his straight chair jam to the bed and pressed a thumb to his father's pulse—little fidgets, bursts; more like static than rhythm, perfunctory life. His own eyes had shut and he'd felt, in that dark quite timeless space, alone and on ramparts, hopeless but still guarding. Then the static had stopped, an instant of wait-ing—no start, no attempt to start, an end. Oh the body had fought—trunk, neck, face convulsed; high squeals in the nose; useless as a headless chicken or snake. He had been standing then to see entirely, hand still on the wrist, when his mother had entered, in innocence, merely checking. Before she could even see the purple face, he had shouted her out—"Go. Go now!" She had quickly obeyed and he'd seen it through alone (the nurse returning a moment after calm had succeeded the struggle).

Now he was blocked from this present ordeal by a

Keep Out sign, behind which nurses were working intensely to keep his mother alive—as what? a mindless hulk, paralyzed, dissolving through endless months. Surely he could stop that, could ring the bell—not for information but to issue orders: "Bring her out. Put her into a room with me. I'll watch till she dies." He pressed the bell. If it rang at all, he could not hear it.

But a nurse came sooner than he expected—tall, handsome, forty. She stood in the door, half-opened, and smiled. "You're Mr. Eborn. I can *see*," she said.

He paused, not understanding.

"—From your mother. You're like her."

That abruptly canceled his force. He could only say, "She's here now, is she?" and point inward, behind the nurse.

The nurse blinked. "The doctor was looking for you. Wait there and I'll tell him."

He knew she was dead and walked to the lounge in that certainty, sat in the empty plastic room and faced the doors. He could only think, "Now how will he tell me?"

The doctor came quickly also, unsmiling. Eborn rose to avoid a hand on his shoulder, but the doctor was taller and the hand descended. "Take it from here, son. She's dead," he said.

Eborn studied the coarse face, said to himself, "He is no more than ten years older than I." The hand pressed him downwards.

The doctor said "Sit" and both of them did—too near, knees touching, on the shallow sofa. "You'll want to call your funeral home next. Have you thought of one?"

Eborn nodded. "Patton's."

"The best," he said. "The best of course. They'll come right here and handle it all." He squeezed Eborn's knee (helpless it shied). Then he stood, stepped back. "I wish I could have helped her."

Eborn said "So do I."

The doctor did not pause to de-fuse that, though he took another step or two—his busy life. "Can I help *you?*" he said.

Eborn stood, nodding fiercely. "Of course you can. You can say where she is—her body, now—and why you would not let me stay till the end."

"It was nothing to see. No pain, no fight. She simply stopped, very quietly, while our backs were turned. Here; then gone. But I'll take you to see the remains if you like—"

"I would," Eborn said and only when the doctor had turned and he had followed, did he understand the verb he'd agreed to use: "If you'd like"—"I would like . . ."

He had seen the body, gray as laundry scum; then gone to the undertaker's, stated firm instructions (she was not to be embalmed and not made-up—the short red man had smiled sad agreement, "We don't doll 'em up"); phoned Ida Nolan, asked her to lock the house (she had had a key these past two years, for emergency); then driven with glazed care the thirty miles towards his study—not towards *home, house* or *Jane* but his present work, the essay to finish. He had not even thought what he'd do if Jane were there—what he'd say to explain his solitary choices, how then to leave her alone with the news, the mass of arrangements. Familiar road blurred past the tunnel of his focused hungry vision as he shaped in his head the final pages; and the paper and ink to set them down (for what?—for *use*) seemed vital as breath; more vital than any person he knew, any temporary duty.

The house was empty. Jane had seen his note. He glanced at hers—*Back to fix your dinner.* It was 3:15. He would have an hour; with luck a little longer. He went to the study and, looking for a moment at his parents' picture (both deleted at last), he read again only the previous sentence—*I have no memory of ever wishing to be anything but an artist. First, a painter; second, a musician; at last, a writer. . . .* Then he wrote through to an end—

But when I had tried and proved to myself that my gifts for painting were insufficient—that whatever my ambitions and delight and despite the contemptuous praise of friends, I could not paint a beautiful picture or sing—then in my last years of school I began to write: first, jewelled love poems; then Poe-esque tales; then at last the seam at the core of my life (richest ore I could offer, however embedded in rock and ice). Stories and novels.
    I wrote from the start with stiff reluctance, difficulty, even pain—more difficulty and pain with each

year—but the sense of excitement, exultation, which paralleled the struggle in fear and hope (and occasionally blossomed for a moment at the end—before flaws and failure hulked into sight), this exultation became its own end and showed me finally that the action which produced this state was surely my work. Was and is. Is because it must be; not because it is my wish or pleasure or source of income but because it is two deeply adamant things—my gift (forced on me by birth and growth) and my need (mined from me, by myself, to make those tools of defense and reconnoiter which my past, present and future demand—shields, mirrors, microscopes, telescopes).

Thus I have worked for twelve years now in the solitude necessary to a writer (which is only, at last, the solitude of all—the solitude which is cause and condition and enemy of work but which only work can arm us against) and have subjected my work to the judgment of an unpredictable, generally uncomprehending public so that I might, first, understand (or at least catalogue) the threatening mysteries of the world, of my human fellows and of myself; second, that I might communicate my understandings, however feeble, to a few other men as baffled and endangered as I by all the controllable and uncontrollable mysteries of the universe, God, human nature.

My work then is what all honorable work is—the attempt to control chaos. It has helped to free me from physical want and from prolonged dependence on my fellows, even loved ones. It has freed me for the attempt to understand, if not control, disorder in the world and in those I love. It has even freed me, though

*for moments only, to round on myself, stand, face my
own failure; and survive the sight.*

He had made that much at least from the day—in
the teeth of the day, from dream to death. Now he was
tired. He squared the four pages in the center of the
table, then went to the couch and stretched flat there.
He shut his eyes and thought, "I will not think, not yet,
not for an hour"; and with the concentration he had
learned in school (to sleep at the heart of a rackety
dorm), he quickly sifted downwards toward sleep—two
layers, three—then was met by something rising,
stronger, which bore him with it to full consciousness.
But he kept eyes shut through a moment of annoyance,
then plunged down again. A solid lake—no entry, no
dent. Eyes open, still prone, he felt the room fill with
pressure around him. Walls, windows, door seemed
instantly sealed; and the space (in which he was now
mere clutter) was pumped full in regular strokes, as by
a heart. Full of what?—he rose to his elbows to see.

Nothing of course. Hot sun slanted through the
window as before. No paper stirred.

He looked to his arm—the curled hairs there were
still as wire. Yet all his softnesses bore the brunt—the
pit of his throat, groins, his temples, eardrums. He
opened his mouth to draw a deep breath; and warm air
rammed in—a solid column—before he had even
begun to inhale. He thought of laughing—short, in his
nose—but no sound would come. "I am very tired," he
thought. He was also afraid—not of harm but of nearness; the pressure forced inward each pore of his skin.
"I must open the door," he thought; then "Can I

move?" He carefully planned to swing his legs from couch to floor; and when they obeyed and raised him, slightly tottering, he went in quick relief to the door, opened it outward and—grateful—felt the room behind him subside.

"Safe," he thought. "I am very tired." Then he turned, faced a room now as normal as a lobby, lay and slept at once. Deeply.

Dreamed again. He stands at the kitchen sink, stares toward the street, which is as empty as his house and as calm. All his. He seems to lack skin—bounds, limits, walls—seems to fill his own house, yard, road with his calm. A calm he has won and which spreads now, unthreatened. Happiness. He is drinking water. As his head tilts backward to drain the glass, he sees three cars turn into his drive. Three vans stuffed with people. The first two rush up, flank the front steps boldly. All van-doors burst open, strangers burst out—dozens. Swarm the yard, busy midgets, maggots, searching something—food? His feeling is anger, cold rage not fear. He will go to the porch steps, order them out—or demand their business. The third van however has gone a different way—up the side of the house, the garbage-man's track—has stopped closest of all, ten yards from the house. Children rush out, in uniforms—blazers, caps, stockings—mill there in the dry leaves. It's autumn, rain starts; a fine mist, cold surely. The children's heads are bare, their blazers soaking. But he still feels only rage and chooses them, will go out the side door and shout to them. He goes, slams the screen-door behind him for attention. The children do not look. They still face their van, waiting for something. He thinks of what to say, can only think "May I help you?" But he does not speak. The short shelving roof of the side porch has vanished. He himself is drenched, cold. The children swirl around two adults, descending, who at once take a firm lead, strike off for the garden at the back. The children follow, smiling. Their guides are his parents—Eborn's own father, mother; in dark blue raincoats, brisk, sure-footed, unblinking. They do not see him or hear him when he sobs, abandoned, violated.

He woke in late light, Jane standing above him. She was smiling enough to ease him back—welcome, forgiveness, plea for pardon. He concealed his dream, postponed its force; then smiled and yawned; then tested the time through an unshaded window—it was later than he'd planned. Six, maybe seven.

"You're safely back," she said.

It was not a question; but he smiled Yes again, then remembered the day. The dream, then death, then whatever had fought his nap. His head strained up to see the desk—his essay, untouched. "Safe," he said.

She extended an arm.

He took her wrist, accepted her beside him on the narrow couch.

"Back long?" she said.

"Two hours, maybe three."

"You'll never sleep tonight."

"I worked before napping. Slept maybe an hour. I had a bad night."

"So did I," she said. "A terrible dream—house full of guests, all hungry and tired!"

How could he tell her now, atop her joking dream? "*I'm* hungry," he said and began to rub her spine.

"I can feed *you*," she said. "I contracted for *that*."

They waited awhile, both facing the window. He kneaded the small of her firm back, quite deeply. "Then feed," he said. He had really meant food and a change of scene (the dream and the earlier assault forgot)—no way to tell her here and now.

But she bent to his lips.

He accepted, kissed her, said "Food, not love." He smiled broadly for her and stirred to rise.

So she rose before him. "Five minutes," she said. "It's in the oven." Then she went to the door, paused, faced him again. He was on his feet. "Your mother's message. I've worried all day. What was it, Tom?"

He faced her, blank and white as cheese. "Oh Jesus, I do not know," he said, entirely hopeless.

TWO

AFTER her funeral, the last two weeks of college were welcome. Final lectures were still, for Eborn, final *chances*—to say, to show, that poems might be at least as useful as roads or loves and as durably made. So in all his classes he had only adhered to previous plans, said the things he had said for eight years past, yet found them wide and sufficient channels for his present force.

He reminded his class in Narrative Prose of the warning he'd issued nine months before—that their effort would be (and, now, had been) not to learn to write but to make a beginning, if nothing more, on the comprehension of their own lives and others'; to grasp, however rudely, the tool of language and begin to bend it into weapon and probe—against what? *uncertainty*: death, loss, betrayal. (They had listened closely; a girl's eyes had filled—not the girl he'd have chosen.)

For his genre class in poetry, he had focused on the final poems of Keats the backward light of Keats's notion of Negative Capability (formed by Keats at age twenty-two, in a letter to his brothers, 1817, three years before his death, eight months before his first hint of consumption—

I had not a dispute but a disquisition with Dilke, on various subjects; several things dovetailed in my mind,

& at once it struck me, what quality went to form a Man of Achievement especially in Literature & which Shakespeare posessed so enormously—I mean Negative Capability, *that is when man is capable of being in uncertainties, Mysteries, doubts, without any irritable reaching after fact & reason.*

At the end he had simply read them *To Autumn,* its open-eyed surrender to death all but incidental to its careful picture of a world after harvest, yearning for end—

> *Then in a wailful choir the small gnats mourn*
>   *Among the river sallows, borne aloft*
>   *Or sinking as the light wind lives or dies;*
> *And full-grown lambs loud bleat from hilly bourn;*
>   *Hedge-crickets sing; and now with treble soft*
>   *The red-breast whistles from a garden-croft;*
>   *And gathering swallows twitter in the skies.—*

and had asked them what more perfect, what stronger, exercise of Negative Capability could be imagined?—to see gnats and swallows, be *content* to see them and fix their lives, their dignity, in perfect language; to do one's work above the pink froth of dissolving lungs, age twenty-five. Then he'd read them the lines from Keats's grave in which poor Severn had encased and softened Keats's own quick epitaph—

> *This grave contains all that was mortal of a young English poet, who, on his death bed, in the bitterness of his heart at the malicious power of his enemies,*

desired these words to be engraven on his tomb stone:
"Here lies One Whose Name was writ in Water"

—and had added, "Keats lied. His work, his calm capability, make his epitaph a lie; for which thank his life." (A boy had asked exactly how much the final exam would count in their grades.)

Then exams. Hot drudgery but numbing, soothing. He had nearly sixty exams to read; and he read them as carefully—with markings and stops for references—as if they were sacred guides toward calm. And he read them in his airless campus office, beside a useless fan, because they were one last chance for solitude before the summer plunge into home-life, concession (despite Jane's eight-hour office day); and when he had finished, computed the grades, stored all the papers in case of complaint—done all he could do short of sleeping there; it was half-past ten—he drove through the cooler night to Jane, too tired to feel guilt or expectation.

But the house was dark. Jane's car was there and the house was dark—quarter-to-eleven, a Tuesday night? He felt strong dread. These two weeks in which he had all but lived without her (two weeks?—seven years) seemed suddenly sufficient warrant for disaster—her suicide, murder, abandonment. "She was tired. She's asleep," he told himself as he stopped his car almost touching hers.

But he trotted to the front door. Locked—proving what? that she lay inside asleep or dead or had left in someone else's car. He entered the dark hall, unconsciously sniffing. No hint in the air so he reached for the lamp, switched it once, no light; again, no light. Bulb dead or unplugged. He said "Jane?," stood a moment—silence.

"I cannot offend," he thought. "*Let* me not." Then he fumbled toward the living room, arms out before him. The light there responded, the room leapt round him. He searched it with his eyes. No disturbance, no body. "She's asleep of course." He moved for their bedroom and saw, on the floor beside the sofa, the school magazine—new cover, his essay. Where had she got it? Maybe Cal had come by? Maybe she had gone with Cal for a drink? "She is in bed of course"—he forced himself to think—"She left the hall light on for me and the bulb burned out. You must go to her." He thought it that way, of himself as *you*.

She was on their bed diagonally, as though claiming it all, on her stomach, covered to the crown of her head by only a sheet.

He stood in the doorway, seeing by the stairs light. He would not turn on a stronger light and advance till she made some movement, breathed or sighed. When he was still enough (suspended, in fact), he heard steady breathing and went softly to her, sat on the bed—in the dark but fully dressed—leaned his mouth to her covered ear. "Are you all right, Jane?"

She always woke quickly, startled, gathered; but now she pressed her face further down, buried her features entirely in pillow.

"Jane?" He exposed her neck, brushed it once with

his chin. "Are you all right, I said?"

She turned her profile slowly away.

He leaned to see. Her eyes were open.

"No, I'm not," she said—voice clear of sleep, if she'd slept at all.

"What's wrong?"

No answer.

He pressed her covered waist. "What happened, Jane?"

She was suddenly weeping.

He could not hear but he felt her shudder and gently touched beneath her streaming eyes. It was only the second—no more than the third—time he'd known her to weep. Tears were final humiliation for her—a Roman matron flat to the wall, no visible escape and no way to die. Yet knowing that, he could not rush in with comfort. Close as he was and as skilled at simulation, he could not bend the last ten empty inches and begin repairs. Tears, however rare, were instruments of entry—crowbars, shims. He sat upright; unlaced his shoes; set them under the bed; then took his own pillow and propped himself outside the cover, face forward, at the headboard.

After whole minutes of that, he touched her— again at the waist (she was turned away). "Now why?" he said.

She was able to speak. "Your essay. Cal brought it by about nine, so proud of his issue, his little coup; and when he had gone I read your essay."

"—And dowsed every light and dug into bed?"

"I was mad," she said. She rolled to her back (he withdrew his hand). "Now I'm only scared."

"You're fearless, remember? Scared of what?"

"—That all you wrote is true. That the mean little, dry little rattling black seed in your pretty gourd is what will last."

He laughed—Vachel Lindsay!—but said "Which seed?"

"There was only one, whatever you thought—that we have ourselves (if we're lucky and stay sane) and must love only that."

"Not *must*. Maybe *can*."

"Check," she said. She nodded fiercely, to the ceiling not him. "—Which is why your wife is bawling like a babe."

"I'm sorry," he said. "I never thought it was news. You've read a few books—'We Die Alone.'"

"But I married *you*."

"I asked you," he said.

"You needn't have asked. I loved you."

"Past tense?"

"All right, present."

"But maybe not future?"

She nodded again.

"And that worries you?"

"*Worries?* It only destroys my life—my present life, forget the future." She started a gesture, unthinking, toward the ceiling (her arms flung up) but stopped—no play—and lay in silence.

He knew the rest, had heard it all his life, always from women (his mother, his aunts bemoaning their husbands, a decade of girls with Jane at the end). He felt for a moment like an older boy, a senior adviser in a freshman dorm—every word predictable hours in advance, every answer exhausted—yet the weight of seven years, her dignity, demanded he hand her on in her plea. "How *destroys?*" he said.

"You know very well."

"Maybe not," he said. However he dreaded the next, he must have it.

She had the fiber to say it to his face, and with him above her. She propped on an elbow towards him, looked up. It was neither a lovely nor pathetic posture. She knew that—and knew it was part of her strength. "My life for almost eight years now has simply been you. *Us*, to be truthful—I'm not a nun—or, *you* and what I could do for you, what that did for *me*. It's the life of every woman, barring bitches and whores—no, whores are included; bitches wish they were. You know—janitor, cook, nurse, mother, laundress, yawning thighs. Well, I'm all that but *mother*—or work at being, despite my job. Tom, we are my work."

He nodded. "And I've thanked you."

"You have. You have. But now you say this—stand up and say aloud to the world (or to ten thousand students and teachers, same thing) that your wife is a wasteful dope, a fool; that all women, barring the bitches, are fools."

"You're sure I said that?"

She did not have to think. "Quite sure," she said. "Any woman's work is for dying things—her family. I could leave my little *job* tomorrow, you know; walk out and never think of it again. But my work is us, and where does that leave me?—racing my wheels to haul dying bodies. Tom, look at your mother—"

He actually looked, toward the dimly-lit door. Open door, empty.

"—According to you, she died in misery simply

because she was out of work; because she hadn't been painting or sculpting for the past forty years or stuffing drawers with lady's verse."

"Not out of work. Just honorably retired. She had made me; I'm here." He intended facetiousness, a mild deflation of the rising tone—woman's magazine, Mother's-Day sermon.

"Exactly," Jane said. "But there's no analogy— may never be, Tom." She said it gently and without reproach, though he'd laughed for the first time at their childlessness.

He slumped to kiss her—no other way out—and though, by his choice, they had not made love since his mother's death (since the self-conscious Rabelaisian affirmation that late afternoon, frantic ball-and-socket drill in the face of death), he was roused in a moment, stood and quickly undressed and tenderly began, both of them slow and confident that the limited end for which they had settled (release, calm) would soon arrive; would be earned by their need and mutual effort.

Jane reached her end (or gave a skilled fake); but near the crest, poised to rush downhill, Eborn missed the chance. The moment clicked audibly in his focused brain—that further trying would be mere exercise. The only other options were to stop cold or fake it. For Jane (for the past two weeks, seven years) he pumped on deceitfully, a master at this—the rising rhythm, quickening breath, tightening fingers. She believed him and worked at helping him, so—downing his loathing, the picture that hung in his eyes of them both hitched glaborous together—he all but believed in the moment arriving and, at last, gave his long sighs as though they were pleasure, his rarest gift.

She believed him still, through the cooling-off; gripped his dry slack buttocks and thanked him, twice.

He pressed her in response, then disjoined and rolled to his back beside her.

She reached for his hand and moved against his shoulder, her face to his profile, watching him.

He also watched but no longer the room or his picture of them but a vision of his father and mother, locked to a bed, their joined hips hacking out signals of love as they worked to unite their lovely skins; but as he watched and they worked on happily sure of success, he saw what they could not—their skins deserting, crusting, then rapidly shrinking inwards till they both swung suspended, dry husks still pumping, though they touched nowhere till at last they dissolved into separate directions and only stains remained. An enormous sac round his own heart emptied, a perfect vacuum, cool and killing; and he said to himself all that finally mattered. "I must save them somehow. They made me for this. I must help them—pitiful children—in time."

When Jane rose quietly next morning at seven, Eborn lay on half-sleeping, not wishing to talk. Only when she came in an hour later for her shoes and bag did he look and speak. (She had re-made herself somehow in the night, no help from him.) "I will be going over to home today."

"Wait till Saturday, Tom, and I'll gladly help. It's

too much for you and Ted's bringing Alix here to dinner."

"I'll be back early and I won't start the clearing, but I've got to go through her papers soon. There'll be legal things."

"Tom, do yourself one kindness. Give yourself a day at least. You've just finished classes. You have got to rest, now."

He did not want to tell her and scrape the fresh wound, but he had to clear his way. "What I've *got* to do is work, Jane; get back to my novel; but I can't do that till I've cleared Mother's house, finished that much at least. So I start today."

The house still looked disturbingly clean. Though uncontrollably neat himself, he'd made early peace with his mother's disorder (dishevelment not squalor) and had been, only weeks before, touched by her saying as she gestured toward corners—"One more thing about blindness, Tom—you never see cobwebs." So now, as he opened blinds and light flooded corners cleared at last for the funeral, he felt a little freed, another knot loosened—the house now entirely *house*, no longer his, no more hung with emotion (threat, demand) than his automobile. The chance for disinterest stood in him suddenly, amazingly—"I can clear all this, myself, today."

He bent to the carpet for a scrap of dried mud and, rising, saw a green shoot beneath a small table. He went there and squatted—four inches of ivy had entered the room from the wall outside, threading mortar and boards till it found a crack in the white baseboard and hung there in dimness. He reached to pull it; then stopped, exultant, his throat free from all the hands that had held it. "I am free," he thought. "This has all surrendered."

Surrendered perhaps but not emptied itself. The furniture waited. (He must sort that with Jane, keep the pieces they wanted, offer the rest to his mother's sister, then sell the scraps.) And the hidden spaces—cupboards chocked with dishes, thirty years of jelly glasses; every drawer a pressed bale of worn clothes or paper. Through all their moves, his mother had carted the mounting waste with a tender passion, not souvenirs but evidence—of time survived, small victories. But they held no secrets, the family papers—all the bank stubs, paid checks, pictures, letters, clippings. He was calmly sure of that already, though before as a boy he had known they concealed hurtful killing facts (they were kept in his youth in a green strongbox), the facts any child suspects he must face—that he is not the natural son of his parents but an orphan who may yet be abandoned again; that his parents' present screens a shameful past; that the faces they show him, bland and smiling, are precarious masks over loathing and glee, mere glazes of love which will instantly melt if he moves once falsely (the rules are not given!), showing hatred, bared teeth. Now he knew they were safe. His mother had brought them out at his father's death, rummaged once through them, then left them unlocked for the rest of her life. No secrets of course, though he'd still not searched them. Two candid lives. The masks had been the faces.

In the surge of relief, he thought of destroying them now, today. A simplifying fire. He'd established, a day before the funeral, that his mother had set them in some crude order (when? and why?)—unpaid bills on top, oldest first; then formal documents (deeds, policies); then the hundreds of letters rubber-banded together; other bundles for clippings and curios (World War II ration books, his curls and shed milk-teeth); a shoe box of photographs. He went as far as the cabinet where they lay, with that intent—to save the pictures and the still-due bills and burn the rest, unopened, unseen; walk out of the house today for good (send a mover for the furniture, an agent to sell it).

He would, and must. It could tell him nothing now, make no reply to questions—if he'd had questions for it. He took the first handful.

At the sight of his mother's script, he was stopped. From the floor of his head, the need he had buried two weeks before tore roughly up—his mother's message, *I'll tell him something*, withheld from Jane and, since, from him. He had made a try at reclaiming it—had asked Ida Nolan, asked his mother's sister at the funeral. They had offered no help. And he'd searched her checkbook, her cash, her debts. She had been near the bone as always but not broke, not low enough even to ask for the check he had let slide by. So, hopeless, he'd forced the question down. Now it spread like hunger at the sight of food.

He sat on the floor beside the stuffed cabinet and again went slowly through her meager accounts. No bill larger than fifty dollars and none had come in since the funeral; her policies, the mortgage, kept neatly to date; a deed to the house (which was still not hers); her exchanges with the government for disability pay (claim still pending)—all her meaningless incompletions, the only unfinished business of a life which had surely finished twelve years before. But that was no news, not from her at least—nor, surely, were any of the other pounds of paper.

He piled them quickly but neatly beside him— dozens of letters from himself to home, in his slowly forming hand (miserably from summer camp; distractedly from college; fully censored from Europe and, in recent years, mere coverings, wrappers for the monthly checks). They must certainly burn—all traces of himself, once committed to writing, lasted only to taunt and humiliate his future.

Then another four letters from his father to his mother—same year and paper as the one he had read by her bed that day. More of the poison that had paralyzed them both from the start—*You are mine, I am yours. Can't we understand that and make each other know?* He laid them with his own. They had done their work.

The next few letters were addressed to his father, in a hand he did not recognize, postmarked 1936. He opened the first—coarse cheap yellow paper, one oddly-folded page, blue-ink, a nineteenth-century hand, manly and leaning and straight-lined at first; then after four lines dissolving into wildness, steeply downhill towards illegibility—

Home
Thursday

My precious Todd
I was never so hurt in my life as I was when the whole week passed and not a word a line nor a sight of you. When the news of Jim's passing came on Monday I

could hardly wait for work-hours to close so you could
get to me. I wanted your arms around me. But have
only had distress. Jim loved me so. I need some money,
5 *if you can spare it and less if not. You forget you said*
you would find me some kindling. The girls are treating
me all right but they will not talk to me enough. Write
at once and come when you can. Stand by me son.

All love
Mother

His *father's* mother, whom he only recalled (he'd been
three when she died, the year of this letter) as ancient
and breathless, always in bed; yet her letter now in this
dim room as airless as her own seemed a letter from
Lear in Lear's own hand, Lear's logic a moment before
the heath (headed simply *Home,* no question which
home; "Home is me, come to me, stand by me—*Oh*
reason not the need!"). She attached herself, a mouth
to his throat, toothless, warm—thirty years dead and
never his; no picture of her ready in his head; but living
now, at his great expense. He at last understood what
he'd known for years—that incest and matricide are
one forged axe, two-handed, two-edged.

As is the past. This paper—these papers he'd
calmly stacked round him—seemed his own lethal past
(or coiling to become that), seemed the objects, the
ends of his parents' lives (their parents before
them)—fierce dedication to dependency, and dependency on things, at last mere paper—the tiny mortgage
on a four-room house (foreclosed, his father unable to
pay); the payment-book on this larger house, still serv-
ing though empty, still unpaid-for and the payers dead;

the soft and desperately genuine lies of a boy's love letters (the boy, the girl—crushed, diseased, now dead); a mother's dissolution into hot senility. Paper had fueled all that wasteful pain. Only paper survived, still potent, unconsumed.

It would not survive him. He stood, took a large trash-basket from the corner and quickly stuffed it—the letters (his own, his father's, grandmother's—all); all the canceled documents; all but the pending bills and photographs (spared now because the box was closed). Then he went through the kitchen down shaky back-stairs, through the yard already nine-inches in grass, to the rusting can.

He was entirely urgent but that included care. The bottom of the can held stagnant rain. He set down his own trash, tipped out the water, then shook in the paper—slowly, loosely, so that each page would have its own air as fuel. Then he leaned in and laid three burning matches at the edges. Their dryness seized fire furiously.

Eborn walked ten yards to a high growth of weeds and hunkered there, pulling, for the time he knew the fire would need. When he rose to look, he had known correctly. A stick in his right hand, he stirred the ashes. They were only ashes, not an unburned scrap. He threw on the weeds to smother sparks; then returned to the house (now safe, still and spacious as a field swept of mines); took the handful of necessary papers, the box of pictures; locked the door and left—a lighter man, stripped by force of will, scraped clean as a keel, aimed for his work.

*   *   *

He thought of his work from the time the wheels moved. That, in itself, seemed an instant recovery, a better omen; for he almost never could think of his work, the unfinished story or novel at hand—agonize, yes, or occasionally gloat or, rarest of all, feel lifted, borne, by a ten-line stretch that simultaneously created and met his full, yet to-then undiscovered, intent; but sit at a desk (or stand or lie) and plan in the blank space behind his eyes, consider all options, the peaks and pits, without making a line, committing a word— that he seldom managed. He did not deeply mind. Oh occasionally in bone-dry stretches, he would ache to *think* his way ahead, to stare into space, a metaphysician, mind clear as Greek air, till the slim probe of reason could consciously pierce its way to order, completion. But on the whole he had made this peace with his faculties, this surrender to afflatus, imperious self-willed, self-serving light—here for minutes, dead for days.

Now, as he drove—papers by him, tame as dogs—he made in his head, sufficient room, the entire centerpiece of his novel, scene yielding scene in an order so rich, so lean-limbed, so beautiful in motion, as to guarantee final light, comprehension, truth. He'd followed enough lies to know one now—and mostly in time. No deceit, no lie could draw him on thus. He had chosen the subject because it was true and because he knew he could end it truer—the first time he'd based a story on "life," directly imported a situation. A woman (a young wife) attempts suicide—a serious try, deep cutting, much blood—but fails and survives. Her husband chooses what she's powerless to choose, to make her live—why? and how? Not himself and Jane but a distant cousin of Jane's who had died. They had gone to her funeral two months before, during spring vacation; and, meeting the husband (a small pressed man), he had suddenly thought, "This is not the ending. What if she had lived? Make her live. Live with her." He had quickly written the first fifty pages—the whole slow day of the girl's decision, her act, the man's finding her, the first rush to save her—physical life. Then he'd stopped, been stopped by the weight of teaching and by his own wish not to let his natural speed plunge him on too soon, his skill in advance of his understanding. Now he knew and could. He raced toward that through the hot afternoon.

But as he rounded a long country curve, he saw a wreck—not the impact itself (he'd missed that by instants) but the car accordioned against a light-pole on his side of the road, not ten yards ahead, its engine still roaring, sparks flying from the tail. He slowed, no other car involved, no cars approaching. One house in sight, set back in woods. It was his to face. He pulled to the shoulder a little ahead and, before he left, laid papers and pictures beneath the seat.

Then he walked quickly back to the roaring car, leaned in at the open window and reached between a slumped body and the wheel to the switch. He had stopped the engine, the showering sparks, before he thought, "That was for myself. It would soon have exploded."

Then he found himself—having walked not run—across the road in high grass, safe now he'd done his unthinking heroics and paralyzed. "Behind the wheel of that crushed Renault is a man. The wheel is in his groin. I did not see blood though I must have touched him"—he studied his hands; they were still their own color. "He is either dead or I must not move him"—he should have thought that as justification but he did not. He stood, five yards away, staring at the car, at what was visible of the trapped man—a high-thrust shoulder, the plane of a neck. It was hot afternoon—he felt that finally—cars would be streaming past with help, with company at least.

But no cars showed, no sound of their coming. "I am trapped," Eborn thought, "as closely as he." He actually pointed, at the end, to the body.

Then he went forward, shuddering; leaned in again, found the man's left wrist and probed for a pulse. Was there a faint occasional thud or was that his own fear? The flesh was warm. Eborn lightened his touch and waited to know. He was looking now over the roof to the trees, the one house there. No sign of life, there or here. His hand touched wetness, his fingers seized. He forced a look inward.

Beneath the slewed wheel and the silent wrist, the man's full groin was sopped in blood.

He drew out, to leave. Leave for what?—help or flight? He did not know but he'd stood fully, taken three steps toward his car, when a distant voice said, "I've called the patrol. Shall I call an ambulance?" A woman's voice. He stopped, strained to see.

She stood in the open door of the house fifty yards away, behind screen wire—a shape, no features.

"Yes," he said.

"Anybody hurt?"

"Yes."

"Any dead?"

He said "I'm afraid."

He had meant "Afraid *yes*" but she said, "Don't be. You're innocent. I saw it all. I'll testify."

"Thank you," he said as though that were in question, as though his face were coated with blood not his fingers. He stood in his tracks and waited for her.

But she did not so much as open the screen though she stayed there dimly in place, behind.

He was halfway between his own car and the wreck. The highway patrol was five miles ahead. How could he wait that five minutes here? "Can you help?" he said.

She thought a moment. "I have done what I can. I am carrying a baby."

He strained again—her arms were empty and straight at her sides, no child at her skirts. Oh *pregnant* she meant. The child would be marked. So he must wait.

He waited where he could, there between the cars, standing, facing west, away from the wreck toward the hill over which he expected help. If the woman stayed on at her door, she was silent. The only sound, barring birds, was leakage—an unbroken stream of liquid pouring from the car to the ground. Gasoline, surely, but he could not look. He scrubbed his fingers on his clean pants leg and said to himself in several forms again and again, "If he is not dead, he must not be moved. I would puncture his heart" (*would* not *could*).

* * *

A patrolman was there in perhaps three minutes. His oncoming car bloomed over the hill before Eborn even began to hope; but the visible quarter-mile between crest and here seemed to multiply beneath him; Achilles and the tortoise, he could never arrive. But he flanked them at last, went a little beyond, slowly not looking, and began a wide turn that stopped him quietly behind the wreck.

He stood and at once went forward to the car, a man in his late forties, older than most patrolmen, safer-looking. He leaned to the body, his head near the man's, one hand plunged in; then never having looked to Eborn said "Help me"—no question that Eborn had help to give.

He came up to give it and saw the patrolman's hand still at the man's wrist—alive or dead? Eborn did not ask and was not told.

The patrolman withdrew—"Let's get him out. Help me break off the door." The door was open six inches but jammed. The patrolman took it in both large hands, pulled powerfully. The car rocked deeply, the man's head bobbled, rose and stayed upright—but not around, did not face round.

Eborn stood in place, staring at the head—short ash-blond hair, a broad unblemished neck. The hair—that surely—had struck him broadside. This was someone he knew—who? surely a friend, some old friend he had not seen for years.

The patrolman pulled again, head rocked again.

Eborn thought, cold as glass, "I have stood and let him die. All my dreams are true. They do not fail."

The door did not yield. The patrolman said,

stronger, "Help me please."

Still watching the unbroken curve of hair—the skull, at least, whole—Eborn also pulled. The door gave, loudly broke at its hinges, folded back. The face still averted.

The patrolman said, "If you'll go around to the other side and straighten his feet, I can pull him out from here. He'll have to come this way, to save his head."

The legs were slung to the far side and pinned. Going there would mean facing him. Eborn said "Please—you," and gestured him round, "I'll pull from here"—from the shoulders backwards into the road, the face still hid. For all his calm past encounters with death, he could not imagine being ready, now or ever, for what must come next—sight of the boy's face which he had condemned, through what?—fear? indifference? (for Eborn thought of him now as a boy, a friend of his youth, no longer a man).

The patrolman obeyed, went silently round, opened that far door, leaned in to the boy.

Eborn watched the man's face as he took the sight—no trace of knowledge, revulsion, regret.

But the patrolman spoke to the boy, "I will need to hurt you now to get you out."

The boy moaned once, what seemed a refusal, which Eborn read as "Leave me here; this was chosen for me."

The patrolman's hands, sufficiently strong, braced themselves against dashboard and seat, forced three inches of room; then quickly worked the trapped legs loose. The boy had surrendered, not moaned again.

But the boy was alive—had been, that moment—and his faint signal freed Eborn fully to join the rescue.

The patrolman looked up and said, "Pull him to you slowly."

Eborn took the shoulders, turned them broadways to him, worked his hands deep into the dry armpits and began to pull.

The boy moved easily; the patrolman crawled behind on his knees across the seat, holding both the ankles. Then when three-fourths of the body was out, the patrolman said, "Can you take the weight?"

Eborn nodded he could—he had taken it already, borne it all from the start. Now that he knew that, his fear was gone. Whatever face, he could bear it now.

And when they had carried the boy to grass, laid him gently there and Eborn had stepped round and seen the face, he bore it of course though even with the eyes shut, nose and lips bleeding, it seemed a face only just concealed in his memory. He leaned closer, studying.

The patrolman squatted and said to the boy, "You're out now, son. Help's on the way. You'll be all right."

The boy moaned again but did not move.

The patrolman looked to his watch, said to Eborn, "Ambulance should be here any minute."

All the blood was fresh, did not dry or brown but renewed itself—the face, the groin. Through thick denim jeans, the genitals seemed to be rendering like pork, not fat but blood.

Eborn said, still standing, "Should we try anything?—a tourniquet—now?"

The patrolman had unhooked the boy's wide belt, undone the waist button, when the boy said "No," weakly but clearly and made his first movement. He raised his right hand with surprising speed and firmness and rubbed at his nose—rubbed it aside, a full inch askew. The flesh at the base had been neatly torn. Now the white cartilaginous septum stood bare in a filling hole.

The patrolman, not pausing, with two gentle fingers swung the flesh back to cover, held it there and said to Eborn, "Hold down his arms."

Eborn squatted on the other side and held the boy's arms. Through cloth, they were cold and the right hand strained to rub again; but Eborn held it firmly without great force.

The boy moaned once more, in what?—protest? pain?—though the sound was weaker.

The patrolman's hand drew back from the face, took the left wrist from Eborn, waited a moment, then said to the boy, "Are you Catholic, son?"

The boy nodded "Yes," not otherwise moving, eyes shut, arms slack.

"Then say an *Our Father*." The patrolman stood.

Eborn looked up to him and mimed with his eyes—"Is he worse?"

"He's dying." The patrolman said it aloud.

The boy had begun a steady sound like a frail wire spun through his purple lips, high and diminishing.

Eborn had had no answer from him, had asked him nothing, offered no word; yet he was the one nearest him now as he had been at first, alone and failing. The patrolman had jogged off towards his own car. So Eborn bent, eight inches from the face, and said "Who are you?"

The sound continued, seamless though finer.

He tried again—"I am Thomas Eborn and I beg your pardon. I could not help because I did not know." Footsteps—the patrolman's—were coming near; but the moan broke off before he arrived, in midair, no fall. The shut face rolled a little toward the ground, the pulse beneath Eborn's finger ended. A stage-death, no struggle, no gagging, no fear.

The patrolman had gone for his black rubber coat. He leaned over Eborn now to warm the boy, then saw, stood erect.

Eborn still held the arms, at the uncovered wrists. He looked up and said to the patrolman, "Who was he?" (meaning "Find his papers. We must notify someone").

Skin like ashes, the patrolman said, "You were here before me. Tell me. Tell me."

Eborn thought, "I am in far over my head."

But a clear voice reached them—"He is innocent." Both men looked to the source—the house.

The woman stood on her high narrow porch, having seen and judged it all from the start. Now she'd dared her unborn child this far. She was only a girl, tall with loose dark hair; and she leaned her great weight against a black railing.

The patrolman said to her, "I know that but thank you"; then started up towards her.

Still squatting, his hands still pressing the boy (for now, cold and white, it was clearly a boy, eighteen at most), Eborn thought, "I am trapped again. In a net I have made of fear and delay, guilt, the service of others."

He drove himself home as though he were glass—the brittlest pane—or as though his car were a powerful magnet which other cars resisted through hurtling luck that would fail any moment and yield his easy death. He strained not to think—of the dead boy; the woman; his name, as witness, in the hands of police; least of all, his novel that, minutes ago, had filled him, buoyed him, promised, like clear water. Instead, he focused his sight and his skills on concrete road, white and yellow lines, signs, lights, bristling junctions—each the possible site of his imminent death, his hundred-and-sixty pound contribution to the daily meat-take of summer roads (each mile thickly pasted with exploded dogs, cats reeling pink gut; the clear sky a sea of whirlpooling vultures). Cold fragility, huddled, at the mercy of objects.

But when he had reached his own green street, his concentration surrendered to what had waited, compressed—"I am willing these deaths and my will is obeyed." The dream, before his mother's death—of Ted and his students wrecked and lost—had seemed fulfilled in her hemorrhage, a black allegory but ended at least. Yet the omen had reopened, metastasized, in today's dead boy, an intimate stranger. When would it close, life proceed unthreatened, not darkly planned? "When I let it," he thought. "When I've stripped all attachments from myself; stand clean of my family, friends, hindering strangers; stand alone, my own."

At the sight of his house, Jane's car in the drive, he shook himself—a wet dog, briefly dunked in madness. But when he had safely stopped and killed the engine, he looked to the floor—the few saved bills and the box of pictures—and thought once more (untouched by regret for the barrel of ashes), "That much is done. Now I breathe new air. My life begins." And though he felt sane and firm and ready, he walked to the house with an old man's care—eyes on his slow feet—and wobbled a moment on the top porch-step.

And at dinner that night with Jane, Ted his colleague and Ted's wife-to-be, he saw as if through the thick lens of age, clearly but coolly, from decades away—Jane opposite him in a blue linen dress, broad-faced, full-lipped, blond hair parted in the center, drawn back. A girl (aged thirty-three) he'd known all his life, had grown up beside but now beyond reach, receding from him with a silent rush. Or was it she who moved? Surely it was he?—but receding or advancing? departing or arriving? from what to what? He watched her now intently, a still point from which to plot his own motion. She had not looked to him for three, four minutes.

Having sensed at once that he would not talk (he could not speak of the wreck tonight though it clamored in his mouth), Jane had taken the slack and was telling a story to Ted and Alix, who both listened gravely—two feet from her lips—as though she were giving clear patterns for life which any fool could follow.

Eborn also strained to listen but could barely hear. Her voice washed to him in crests and troughs, across finished plates, two candles, five feet of teak-table—

"—Had known one another from the start of course, grew up two blocks apart, riding bikes and skating, as plain to each other as two sheets of glass—and no less clear. Not a secret in sight, hearts open for inspection. But lacked curiosity—it must have been. Took for granted in each other things most people die without finding—perfect loyalty, merciless honesty—"

Eborn looked to Ted and Alix, who were still watching Jane not one another, and thought, "Of course. She's describing them. They will soon see that." From his distance, their lives seemed simple, slow, of contemplable size like moving cars from a plane miles high.

"—Then I was in Europe four years later, looking round alone (and beginning to feel my age, twenty-five); and some boy from Alabama stopped me in the street and said, 'Thank God, an American. Speak me some English.' It was only Hamburg and stuffed with Americans, but he was lonely and took me out for beer that night. Some charmless cellar made of unpainted concrete—a former bunker maybe. And the boy sadly turned out to match the place, so I went off-the-air, just nodding now and then to his endless autobiography. Then Tom walked up and was sitting beside me before I completely recovered myself. I could not say his name to the Alabama boy! It would just not come, after all those years; so he introduced himself and at once saw the corner I was in with the boy. The boy said to Tom,

'Are you on a tour?' Tom said 'A *unique* tour.'—'What kind is that?' Tom said, 'A cloud tour. I am looking at unique cloud formations in fourteen countries in twenty-eight days.' Then Tom said to me, 'Are you on a tour?' (The boy had neglected to ask me that, having found me alone.) I said I was. The boy said 'What kind?' Before I could think, Tom answered for me—'A *behind* tour. She's making a survey of unique behinds in all of the leading galleries of Europe.' So I knew he was mine—or would have to be, if I'd have a life at all." She waited, laughed a little—"*Tom*, I mean. Not poor addled Alabama."

Though Eborn tried, fixed on her, to understand—to place her story in her life as he recalled it and make some response for the sake of Ted and Alix—he did not succeed and did not see that, there at the end, she had looked to him and smiled. In the strain of trying to hear, from his distance, and focus mind and eyes, he had found only one fact—that *he* was the mover, not she nor they. Now, in Jane's silence, he said to himself, "I'm receding not running. It is by my own choice and I control the speed. I have had a bad day, I am very tired, and tomorrow I must work." But even his new work would not come to mind—his fresh plans, the subject, the plain idea.

The speed had quickened and when Ted turned, grinning broadly, and said, "Is that your story, Tom?," he suddenly saw that, miles below—in the presence of strangers, silent and hunched and misconstruing—Jane had flapped out her heart like a cheap bolt of goods and called it his also.

He yielded to what he'd begun at last—full flight

not recession, not strategic withdrawal. Eyes open in the room (on the table, on three forms), he saw only pressure, black against his face; felt no care for these people who cared for him; felt only clenched terror— invisible spore locked in frigid mineral of meteor, alive and potent for larger life but trapped and hurtling with only two hopes: impact and explosion or perpetual fall. His cold mouth said to the room "I am sorry." Then he managed to stand, leave and find his bed.

Jane gave him three minutes, then came up to him. She shut the door behind her (Ted and Alix were loudly clearing the table), sat by him on the bed and said "Thomas, what's wrong?" in a tone that granted something genuinely wrong but also granted his right not to say.

Eyes shut, not touching her, he said again "I'm sorry"—all he knew to say.

"But you're not sick?" she said. She pressed his temple.

He shook his head No.

"Bad day though?" she said.

"A very bad day. You warned me, didn't you?" He still did not face her.

But she smiled towards him. "I wouldn't say *warned*. I stated my opinion that you were at least half-human and had run all spring and should pause for air."

He nodded. "I'm pausing now. Or being paused."

She touched his head again—his hair, stroked it back. "Will you come down again?"

"Let me think," he said. "If I don't, say I'm sorry. Say I'll almost surely live till the wedding." (Ted had asked him to stand as Best Man, in July.)

She quietly left him, one dim light burning; but when he had heard her downstairs again and talking calmly, he could only think what he'd offered three times in the past five minutes—"I am sorry." For what? All he knew was the answer; no antidote yet, no reparation. "The wreck, that boy—the woman was right of course. My hands are clean. I am not mad yet. But coming today, the wreck was an emblem of my own cruel waste. Surely not intending it, the boy very easily demolished himself. My act was intended, but easier still. In an ashcan fire I destroyed all I had of my parents' lives, denied them the dignity of their passions. The boy is my parents, may also be me. Mistakes can be permanent. Perhaps I've destroyed what cannot regrow; hacked all of us—Father, Mother, me and therefore Jane—loose from our only tether, the past; our proofs of a constant need and use for love, however less strong, less lasting than our skins the love must be." That seemed the thing he was sorry for, the wreck against which these past weeks had warned him— dreams, his mother's death, Jane's instant discovery of the hole in his essay; then the boy's death, too late, mere confirmation, mockery of his waste. But the thing was done—his own life free and, worse, adrift; his parents' lives fouled and stopped by him.

He opened his eyes so as not to face them; but they stood—in his head of course, he knew—in the dark corner, gaunt, mainly eyes and mouths. The hungry dead.

Odysseus in Hell. For years he had had it by heart and not known why—Circe's instructions for questioning the dead. He shut his eyes and said it, barely aloud—

First, pray from your heart to the empty dead.
Promise that if you find home,
You will burn them a heifer on a pyre of treasures.
Promise Teiresias your black ram, unmarked.
Next kill a black ram and ewe.
Press their bleeding throats to the ground
But you face Ocean.
Then the hungry dead will flock to eat.

He also remembered the rule of Teiresias—

Feed blood to a ghost, he will answer you truly.

Odysseus had obeyed in perfect detail; and the dead had talked—his own mother lapping at the bloody ditch, then telling him all that had happened in Ithaca (his wife, son, father still waiting, numb with grief), then three times evading "like shadow or dream" her son's embrace.

It seemed to Eborn now a fatal error in the truth of the scene—that the dead should speak for sheep's blood only. Too easy a gift. "Heart's blood," Eborn thought. "His own hot life. My own."

But how, short of literally cutting his throat?—and then what use would the dead's news be? (Most of the world's rites and monuments were efforts at answers— food for the dead, so the dead would speak. Speak of what?—their knowledge, plan for our future, hold on our present, which they easily steer.)

For a start, he could stand—in his own safe house (more than half paid-for)—and go down to his wife and friends he'd abused. Temporal but here, under his roof now, and at his invitation. He had asked them in; they'd agreed to come and had tried to come not empty-handed.

He stood and walked to the bureau mirror to comb his hair. It was all in order; and he thought of Jane's smoothing it minutes before as he lay, a self-surrendered fool. A single act in which, unthinking but instant, she'd performed three services and filled three needs, sensual, spiritual, practical—"Let me touch you, Tom (whom I both crave and love); let me set you straight for your certain return."

The return was muffled—descent to an empty living room. Jane was on the porch. Ted and Alix were in their car at the curb. Eborn stopped at the screen door.

Jane heard him and turned. "They are leaving, Tom." Her voice was neutral. If Tom was well, he could urge them back; if not, wave them on.

He stepped to the porch and forward to the steps but did not go down. Closer than this would require explanations.

Alix already faced the road through her glass; but Ted's face waited, turned to Eborn.

So he gave a little balked apologetic wave and said again "I'm sorry."

Ted nodded unsmiling. "Got to work anyhow."

Eborn said, "Good luck. When can I see your poems?"

Ted smiled. "Anytime."

"I'll look forward then." Eborn glanced to Jane beside him, then to Ted again. "Did she give you my message?"

"—That you'd live for the wedding? You will," Ted said. Alix leaned over grinning and they rolled away.

Inside again, Jane asked him only "Coffee or something?"

He extended a hand, splay-fingered—"No, I'm steady and I mean to sleep tonight."

"You will," she said, "—the day you've had." Then she went to the kitchen to finish there.

He sat in his chair and reached for the paper. Under the paper and previously hidden was a manuscript in a black binder. Not his. Something Jane had brought from the press? He took it—Ted's poems, finally gathered and typed. Ted had just now said he could see them anytime. An emblem of Ted, to have left them here, subversive and smuggled—offered if found; if overlooked, lost.

Eborn's first emotion was exasperation—unprofessional; the things could have lain there ignored for days (he had offered to send them to his publisher)—but as he leafed back toward the title page, a loose sheet (folded once) fell to his lap.

For a friend, his dead mother

The times I saw her—two or three?—
In her last wobbly years, she was never at home.
The first time, at work, she sold me a sleeping-bag

(When I unrolled it and asked "Room for two?,"
She rallied—"Anybody you can handle, fits in here");
And a time or two in the Surgical Ward,
Head bald as Khrushchev's (comparison hers);
But not at home—in the place, in herself.

She hung round herself, an old pet evicted,
Cowed at the curb, beneath scrub bushes;
Baffled, a little stunned but waiting—
Permission to weave toward familiar rooms,
Signal from a source she could not remember
To slough off sixty pounds, recap blown veins,
Scrub caul from her eyes, stand again in the place
She had most enjoyed, her obedient body—

A girl who has weathered an orphanhood,
Daily props a soaked husband through the endless
  Depression,
Curves this moment on the day-old son
Her body has built in less than a year
From pork liver, canned milk, hominy.
He need not grin, may foul his can,
Scald her hands in ammonia. She bears that lightly,
Being where she belongs.

I welcome her there.

Ted had made his try, which Eborn knew, for the
first time now, he'd expected since Ted failed to show
at the funeral or make the least word of allusion to the
death. Ted's way—an act, slow and carefully prepared,
offered all but anonymously, yet so graceful in its large-

handed urgency as to shame most others. Eborn most of all. Knowing that the thought was the last Ted could have, Eborn felt condemned by the quick plain picture, the thin but piercing vision of her life—condemned in his own baroque retreat, his filigree shields that had shattered at a touch.

Yet he also knew that, like most poems, Ted's was less than true, lovely not beautiful (the Bethlehem Mary, not the baffled widow of Nazareth, abandoned), translucent not clear—not all the truth by any means on that single subject, any more than *Lear* covered all its ground. Hobbled by verse (the form itself, its mandatory pitch, its loose elliptic grip on time) both Shakespeare and Ted were finally excluded from the total discoveries available only to donkey-prose, the longer journey, diurnal haul.

"My mother's life was larger than this. But how? Prove it"—that flicked into Eborn's head as suddenly as all his previous motives for work. Work which brought with it instantly the promise to anchor his own flapping life, repair his parents' he had tried to destroy, discover in their lives the available truth they had died without—and endure without (the lives of his parents being now at his mercy). Food for the dead, so the dead might speak, be spoken to.

When Jane had finished and come from the kitchen and waited in the door, he was able to see her steadily—a girl not sure she was not alone. He thought, in a rush, "She is not alone; I will stay here, and need her." He could not say it—a blockage, of tenderness, plugged his throat.

She gave him time, demanding (no, allowing) that

he name their future effort, tone, rhythm—tonight, years to come.

He was able to say, after swallowing, what she no longer felt the right to say, "Shall we call it a day?"

She shrugged but smiled, gladly feigning fatigue— "Nothing else to call it."

Then he stood to join her.

THREE

The next morning, once alone in the house, Eborn cleared his desk of all but clean paper and the one photograph which had waited for years—his father and mother, young, on their bridge. Then he began—that easily, with the mild elation of any beginning but none of the dread (no sense of a finish delayed years from now; the mouth of a tunnel) and no plans or notes. He wrote as if transcribing, not inventing at all, though the photograph and odd small memories were his only guides and documents—

IMAGINARY SCENES FROM THE LIVES OF MY PARENTS
1. THEY MEET. *February '23*
Known: *That they met at a frozen pond, each having come with someone else.*
Imagined:
She has never before seen a pond frozen hard. (There is no pond within five miles of Markham her home; only one narrow creek, and in seventeen winters—she is sixteen this month—it has never frozen.) So she does not skate. And will not try, knowing no one here, ten miles from home and sick at the thought of an ugly try in the presence of strangers. The boy who has brought her—Albert Riddell—has given up begging her and skated off. (He works in Markham; these people are his friends.) But she knows enough about ways to move to know that only one person in the crowd can

skate worth watching. She watches him—from her seat, a snowy rock, on a low wooded rise ten yards from the ice, at the end near the dam. Her thick blue suit, thick stockings, keep her warm—the day is gray—and her coarse black hair, short and swept like struts to cover her ears, does not lift in the wind. Beside her, sunk in the snow, are the skates Albert borrowed for her. She wished, until he left her five minutes ago, she could fling them in his teeth, cut deeply through his grin. (He is twenty-four; no friend of hers; and three-sheets already, at ten a.m.) But now she ignores the rusting skates and Albert and watches the boy—in the center, there, tagged by a tall girl but alone in his ease and certainty as a horse among cows, refusing kin. She notices also that, except for his girl, no others watch him. They wouldn't, this crowd.

She sees his movement only—not his face or clothes or size—and she does not relate him in her mind to other things, other boys or games. What he does, seems all he is—but valuable, singular and irreplaceable.

He thrusts strongly out from the girl his shadow and the tight ring of others till he skims on alone; then leans onto one leg, the raised leg back and straight; rides on that—the force of his single thrust seeming endless, sufficient to fuel any trip he wishes, any trick or turn. (His tall girl quits, pumps back to the others with short hectic strokes.)

How good is he really?—at this, she means. She suddenly wishes she knew these rules, to size him up, judge him (as she could in an instant had he been on a horse). His glide continues, takes him slowly toward the dam—she can hear his blade cutting—and now the others watch him. But he does not turn; he watches the green ice, his steady foot. She knows he is good—that he trusts his skill, his elaborate power so simply displayed, and needs no approval, no witnesses.

A voice yells, "Fool! Stop showing off."

He does not flicker or his motion falter.

The voice is his girl—"Todd, you're aimed for the dam!"

He is, and continues.

The girl lunges out on a rescue dash; in two steps she falls to her face loudly, blood.

He does not turn—has he heard her at all? His movement is slowing though his back leg is steady; then, a yard from the dam (the drop is twelve feet), his shoulders shift rightward and he curls off in time, starts a slow circle round and half-completes it (it could bring him facing her, though twenty yards away). His strength is failing—not his ankles and knees (she sees them, rock-firm) but the force of the stroke. He has not calculated. He will stop short of finishing the end he began.

She is sorry of that, more angry than sorry. She was his witness, need her or not. It is she he has failed —not the girl flopped, knees-spread, there on the ice; her forehead bloody; a covey around her headed by Albert.

He stops. Todd stops. She knows the name from his girl's silly warning. His botched circle leaves him facing the crowd, his girl at the center. He skates toward her, but slowly, not smiling, as though he abandons duties and needs that pull on him stronger than her shallow cut (already half-healed) but from too great a distance—a rock on the rise at the end of the pond, the girl who is suddenly shivering there, black-haired, alone, whom he has not seen.

—And would not see if he looked up now. Too cold to wait—wait for what? day to end—she has walked to Albert's car and sits there low in the driver's seat (she has known how to drive for five or six years; her sister forbids her). It is slightly warm here because of the lantern. Albert keeps a kerosene lantern by the engine when he parks in the cold; she has brought it inside, set it near her feet. Her watch says eleven. The day lies flat and endless around her. She cannot change it, having come this far with a half-drunk fool; she must trail behind till he calls it quits and takes her home or passes-out and leaves her. She would hope for that, except for her sister, her oldest sister that she lives with now—if her sister ever thought Albert took two drinks (much less saw him drunk), she'd be all but chained to the bed for months.

But the day (this miserable day among strangers) has one advantage—it is shorter than her life, will end in hours. At her age, she cannot imagine enduring a natural life. Like all thoughtful children she is desperate—calm but hopeless, no sense of a future. "My life is like this. It is run by others, no word from me. It can never change. They will never change." She has thought that through till it slides like silk thread; something she can say (and has said for years) that is terrible and true but, finally, familiar—the Lord's

Prayer, the Psalms. She huddles to sleep, coat tight around her, collar scraping her ears. And manages it quickly, thank God; no dreams.

She is wakened by "Lou!"—her name at last but shouted from a distance. Stiff with cold, she does not move. No one but Albert. Let him think she's lost. Let him sweat awhile. She slumps deeper inward, lies across the seats, unsmiling at her joke. The voice calls on, down the hill by the lake; and Lou is almost asleep again when a voice—not Albert's—says "Louise Attwater," near and moving nearer. She stays in place. She is waiting again.

"Louise Attwater"—said, not shouted, and with no tone of question; a statement of fact: "Where she is, I will find her."

She lies, eyes open, staring up and backwards at the isinglass curtains, a dirty gray rectangle of sky cut by cedars. She thinks, "Who will find me and why would he try?"

The face is strange and almost frowns but, even upside-down, does not frighten her. She does not rise, remains in the narrow warmth she has made and stares, unrecognizing, up. No man has ever frightened her; she does not expect one ever will; and since her father's death in her arms, she has vowed no man will hurt her again, pierce deep enough again.

He asks "Louise?"

She bolts up and looks—this one is harmless, disarmed in advance; his broad clear face blushes fiercely at her look. She grins, says "Present!" Then "Who wants Louise and why in the world?"

He looks away, toward the ice as for coolness, but stands his ground; only points downhill. "I am just Todd Eborn. Albert Riddell wants you and he'll tell you why."

She looks past him, past his huge pointing hand to the white hill, Albert climbing slowly with the clumsy girl, her head strapped with cloth—this scared boy's girl. "—Want on," she says, "wanting's not getting." Her vehemence shocks her slightly; she laughs.

The boy does not turn; but she studies half his face, not actually studies but wonders mildly—that any boy who can move like that, half-an-hour ago (*the best in the county*) should look as plain from the neck-up as this (*not ugly, not even unpleasant*—usual) and that he could, once off the ice, duck round at the beck and call of a girl fool enough to try what she couldn't (*to save him, on skates, from what he did best*) and then take orders from a half-drunk Albert to track down Lou Attwater, a stranger. She finds she has thought herself near to pity—and for this dumb boy balked at her window. She needs a few answers. "Is your sister really hurt?"

He slowly turns and searches her face for guile; finds it, frankly displayed; and is calmed, the start of a new nameless game, no rules, what goal? Smiling, he says, "I have three sisters, all younger than me, and they all hurt badly. They are home in Prentiss right now blue with cold—and a widowed mother—all waiting for me to come on back and harness-up and feed the fires and their hungry faces; but, no ma'm"—he looks to Albert and the girl; they are just out of range—"this one is no blood-kin. I shouldered her voluntarily."

"—And you're sorry?" she says.

"Broken-hearted," he says. They laugh together—a laugh Lou continues when the other two arrive, though Todd has stopped.

Albert stops three yards from the car to puff; the girl comes on and stops against Todd, a mule at a fence.

Beneath her laugh, Lou thinks, "He is hers. She knows that better than she knows her name."

Todd takes the girl's hand, smooths her fallen hair back to show her face and says to Lou, "This is Sybil Hedden."

Lou swallows the end of her laugh and nods.

Albert steps up and says, "And this is Lou Attwater—blue-ribbon winner on any horse alive but won't hit the ice, been pouting all day."

Sybil faces Lou and nods unsmiling; and Todd, still holding her hand but looking down, says, "Congratulations. Some have been doing both this whole bad day."

Sybil frees her hand and looks to Albert. "Just take me home."

Albert says to Lou, "I'm her second cousin."

Lou thinks "I forgive you" but looks to Todd. He is white with misery. So she says "Me too."

Albert says "You what?"

"Take me home too."

Tears spring out of Albert as if under pressure. (He has had nearly half-a-pint since breakfast.) "Why?" he says.

Lou knows he is drunk, but she tries to spare him. "Because I am frozen."

Albert smiles. "I can warm you."

"—And because I am not doing anybody a bit of good here."

Albert cannot speak. He is all but sobbing.

So Todd says to Lou, "Are you a missionary?"

She thinks and says "Yes."

"—Of what?"

"Well, of plain good sense for one sure thing. Of not making public fools of yourselves, trying what you can't handle, lifting what you can't bear." Lou ends smiling but she means all of them—Todd wasted on this Sybil, Albert on her, she on them all.

Only Sybil understands. She says, to Lou's teeth, "I am walking home. It's not but four miles."

And she's limped five steps before Todd says gently, still in his old tracks, "Go now and you're gone."

When, from her steps, Todd has seen Sybil safe and sizzling through her door and frowned his slow way to Albert's car, Lou intends to say again "Now me" but Todd prevents her.

He opens the door on her side not the back and says to her, "We need you now to chaperon us on a little side-trip we have to make." Then he slides in beside her—no wait for her to move, no question that his new intended place is to share her seat.

She looks to Albert. He is glassily grinning. Then again to Todd—his frown has eased and his clothes touch hers from shoulder to knee; but he does not *smile, so she says "All right" and does not ask where they will go or will end or when.*

She finds, as they start, that it only mildly annoys her that Albert knows. He grins on, mostly at her profile not the road; but she is not with him, any more if ever. Pressed between them in the cold rush of air, she is in a large room—she sees herself: alone as always (these four years at least) and freer than ever in all her life, as abused and hopeless but also waiting. She does not ask herself "For what?" but she feels no fear though she quickly thinks "I should, I should." She cannot. She feels Todd's eyes, unblinking on her. There is nothing he could take she would not calmly give.

Todd is far behind her—oh close beside *but has only begun to see and sense her. His stare meets Albert's across her nose, they both dodge away; but Todd knows that Albert has no claim here. She has not given anyone deed to herself. She is sealed in her clothes, hair, skin; her own. And along their curved narrow line of touch—she to him—she is cold, as she said, and entirely still, her firm lean face high and pointed forward, accepting the road, her black hair unstirred by the stiff cross-wind. But she* moves—*he can see. He studies her, strains to name her motion—tremble? shiver? some hidden pleasure?*

None of them—but idleness *and* energy. *She shudders with both—secretly, invisibly to all but him—the need and readiness to be lighted, burned. But carefully, slowly.*

Todd yearns to cradle her—freezing child—and looks again to Albert who is fixed on the road; so he lifts his left arm, lays it behind her, lets it of its own weight press her neck and shoulders. She accepts the touch and they ride on thus—Todd thinks of to where? no more than Lou knows. Though now he also faces the road, he thinks truthfully, "She is nothing so grand, so out of the way. Sybil is prettier and Sybil is mine. But this girl is here. She has come loose from Albert. It's not yet noon and she says every instant, 'I am game for the day.'"

Todd is right. She is, though like him and Albert she rides in silence, their only sounds being merely sounds—grunts as they sail into skids on the ice, sighs as Albert saves them each time. He is drunk enough to be scared, thank God; so he keeps up a steady careful clip back out of town (not the way they came) though for all Lou knows, they are headed to the pond; still she does not wonder and does not turn one time till he stops, slewing round, in the midst of the road, not a house in sight, thick pines both sides, and says to Todd, half-whispering across her, "She can't go in, not with Ruby there and all; so you sit with her, keep the engine warm right where it is (nobody'll want to pass today) and I'll do the business if you'll cross my palm." He is grinning by then, to Todd not Lou.

But Todd, unsmiling, digs for his purse and hands across her a pill of money (a bill folded down to the size of a dime).

Albert wades through the high snow, strikes into woods at a spot which at first seems impenetrable. But he manages, vanishes.

Lou feels a single moment of guilt—now that she's left him, has never accompanied him, has used him only as transportation for short excursions out of her life. He has asked for that, though; has offered no more. So she slides across to the driver's seat, leans back on the door and says "Who is Ruby?"

Todd smiles, checks the view as though for listeners, then laughs and says "How old are you?"

"Sixteen this month."

"So is Ruby," he says. "But it's still too young." He is smiling but firm.

She says "How old are you?"

"Nineteen, nearly twenty."

She thinks that through, begins to nod fiercely. "Todd Eborn," she says, "you can skate and I can't but that's all the edge four more years give you; that's everything you have got on me, everything that counts (what does skating count?)"—she winces at that last, a rudeness and lie—"I have lived through losses and terrible sights; I live in pain every minute, every day. Sixteen more years like these, I'll be dust—be glad to be."

He can barely hear for watching her, her motion—the same steady flicker as before but quickened, hot, and no longer idleness or readiness. "She's fighting"—he thinks that clearly, beneath her words—"but what? and for what?" So when she has stopped (she stares on at him, a whole new color), he says "What pain?"

She looks around her, at snow and woods. "How much time have we got?"

92

"*Till what?*"

"*Till Albert.*"

"*Time enough for you to tell sixteen years.*"

"*Where's he gone?*"—*at last.*

"*To buy us some liquor.*"

"*You and him, you mean.*"

"*Suit yourself,*" Todd says. "*But it kills all pain, since you're in such pain.*"

"*I have stood my pain on tea and coffee this whole time,*" she says. "*I can limp on, I'm sure, without bootleg liquor.*" She turns from him, stares at the empty road as though testing its strength to bear her weight.

"*What pain?*" he says.

She stays turned away and is silent awhile. Then she draws deep breath and, still not facing him, says, "*Just loss. You say I am sixteen and not old enough to know what drunk fools do for fun (or stone-sober people when the shades are down); but tell me this one thing, Todd, since you know—how come I was old enough at nine to lose my mother and how come at twelve I held my father four years ago and watched him die, a young man, from T.B.? Four years ago and here I sit, broad-side a country road, half-stiff with cold, waiting for the village drunk with a smile on my face. I was what he had—my father, I mean. He was—God knows now if He didn't then—what I had in the world. I'm my sister's now. Something she didn't want any more than me—and wants even less after these four years. 'Be patient,' I tell her. 'Just enjoy my looks. I am gone next year'—this June, I mean, come Commencement Day.*"

"Gone where?" Todd says.

"To my bachelor brother in Baltimore. We worship each other."

"How will that help?" he says.

"If you don't know that, you are too young to learn." She waits another instant, turns on him and smiles—"Who is Ruby?" she says.

"The bootlegger's daughter."

"What's her claim to fame?"

"Her line of work."

"—Which is?" she says.

"Put it this way," he says. "She sells a different brand of joy from her Daddy."

"To Albert?" she says.

"Ask Albert," he says.

"To you?"

He does not calculate. "No," he says. "Too busy, too broke."

"What was that you gave Albert?—counterfeit?"

He is happily caught, grins as though he has lied. "It was what little money I snatch every week from my mother and sisters' hungry mouths for my own ease of mind."

"Money buys you that? Then I'm hunting a banker."

"You've found one—Albert. Just hang onto Albert. He's well-fixed—Albert. Good job, new automobile, savings piled in the vault."

"—But no mind to ease?" She makes it a question to show Todd her leaning. Her thoughts lean to him, her body all but follows, her heart is there.

But he does not look. He remembers a story to

prove her question. "—No mind at all. Remember Ruby we were talking about?"

"Yes."

"He'd been seeing her—out of the side of his eye; Albert's eye, I mean—two or three years, when he'd come for his liquor—from just a little girl on up and out to what she is now; and early this fall, she spoke to him. Or so he said; said she sneaked up on him from behind a tree one evening late as he was leaving and told him her brand of fun was also for sale. He all but swallowed his jar, I guess, and left at a run though he told all of us he was just short of cash—Hell, you know she gives credit." Todd stops and flushes, looks to Lou and says, "Is this too rich for your blood, this story?"

"No," she says. She kills a smile.

"Well, stop me when it is. I live among ladies so I rarely speak to them and don't know the rules."

"I do," she says. "Keep speaking, please."

"What he wanted, of course, was chaperons, a gang around him; so by promising them a bargain deal, he got some boys to ride out with him one Saturday night. He'd arranged with her first—or so he said—that her Daddy'd be deep asleep long before and that she would meet them in the little woodshed. He and his gang went out about ten, left the car out here and walked single-file on the balls of their feet till Albert raised his hand on the edge of the clearing—the signal for him to go first, alone. Well, on he went to the woodshed door and knocked one time. A voice said 'Uh-huh!'; he opened the door and a shotgun went off, both barrels in the dark. The only light was blue—from the gun—and no sound followed the gun, just ringing;

so who knew if Albert was dead or ruined and who'd pulled the trigger?—Ruby or her Daddy? Everybody left of course; ran, to be truthful. But halfway out to the road somebody stopped and whispered to the others, 'Hell, we can't leave him lying.' Somebody else whispered 'Hell we can't' and they all went on. Albert had beat them. He was there in the pitch-dark sucking breath and cranking his car—"

"*Where were you?*" *Lou says.*

"*I'm ashamed to tell you.*"

"*Leading the runners?*"

"*Standing empty-handed in my own back yard.*"

"*Empty-handed of what?*"

"*My liquor I'd bought.*"

"*From Ruby's Daddy just before he pulled the trigger?*"

"*Not that night, no. I have other sources. No, what I had done was ride out of town with a friend of mine and buy my sweet jar with my week's savings. The friend is rich and had bought two jars, so we'd drunk one of his all night and stoned a pond. I was feeling fine when I got home late about two o'clock. My friend drove me up in our back yard quietly—he had cut his lights first—and I was walking in towards my bed, straight and happy; was halfway to the house when the backdoor sounded and here from the dark was my mother, hair-plaited, nightgown to the ground. Well, we knew each other. No light was needed. And she knew her next move. She felt for my right hand and found the cold jar. Not a word, not even a 'May I please?'—she accepted the jar as if it was hers, like everything else my hands bring home. Then she took*

three or four slow steps to the side, to an iron water-
spigot that stands in our yard. I didn't see, didn't try to
see; but I heard her break it as neat as an egg—one tap,
it was ruined; my lovely week I had worked for so
hard."

Lou says "Poor you" in deprecation.

But he does not yield. "No," he says. "I believed
your pain, which you said was loss. You could honor
mine—" He pauses, unfinished; the pause greatly length-
ens.

"—Which is what?" she says.

He knows. She has made him know. "Duty," he
says, "to the people I must love. Some of them I do—"

Lou says to herself, shuddering with the cold they
have both forgot, "I will love him, no question of must,
all my life. I begin this moment."

Todd has partly understood that, despite her silence, having partly willed, gently extorted it. But he
does not speak. It is too soon yet. She will signal when.
And Albert is here, wading slowly through snow, hands
empty, face saddened. Lou's back is to Albert so
Todd tells her softly, "Your last chance for riches is
almost upon you."

She turns; Albert opens the door in tears. "You
were recognized," she says.

He does not even see he has been betrayed. He
speaks to Todd only. "He says I am drunk, won't sell to
a drunk. I'm sober as God!"

Lou has moved to her place on the spare seat with
Todd. She says from there, "You are drunk, Get in.
Sober, you'd have never showed your face there again
for fear of hot death. Crank this car now and drive us
out."

Albert simply nods and heads for the crank; but Todd says, "Give me the money. I'll go."

"I am freezing," she says.

But he's out already, his breath white around him, and frisking Albert's pockets—Albert stands, hands-up, entirely surrendered.

She leans out to Todd and says "Tell me why?"

"To warm you up." He has found the money.

"Take me somewhere then where there's fire and I'll live."

Todd comes to her open window, chuffs through his fist; then he whispers to her, eight inches from her lips—"I'm the one will die, sweet Lou—of thirst and of course my famous pain—if I don't go in there now and close the deal. You wait for me."

Albert has put down the crank and come round to enter and sit.

"You wait," Lou says and flees toward Todd. She will not wait here, could not, is drawn.

Todd permits her gladly, waits; then they walk forward singly—he in Albert's fresh tracks, she carefully in his. (Albert has stayed behind speechlessly, will be asleep well before they have vanished.)

And when they have vanished and tramp ahead through the brief still woods which coldly stroke their faces, it is only Lou who thinks of their solitude, the first time alone, first test of their chance. The walking in snow requires her attention; but she seizes moments to study Todd—his slope-shouldered back, his high-shaved neck—and wonders at her choice yet never doubts. Her single doubt is, "Does he reply? Or will he, when he looks? When he finally sees?" What she most needs now and searches to find is a question to ask—one sentence to say in her natural voice which will not force or frighten him but will pierce and reveal his heart.

No question comes and they are there, the end of the woods, bare house ahead, no human in sight, a dog curled in snow asleep or dead. She sees the woodshed, the house-door shut, and suddenly thinks "Suppose we are shot." The thought is serious not idle or comic; and her first silent answer is "Shoot ahead, I die content." But her new love rises, defends itself—"It would be the worst of all my pains; to die now, happiness two steps before me."

Todd shows no fear, never slows an inch or turns back to Lou for last look or warning. He comes to the five swayed steps of the house, takes them doubly, in stride—the dog never stirs yet is breathing, alive—and knocks four times.

Lou has stayed behind him, stopped on the top step; but when the man comes, it is she he looks to, addresses first—"I don't trade with ladies."

Todd says, "She's no lady. Not yet if ever. And I'll never be. Two jars of your best." His money is out, unfolded on his palm.

The money, his palm, his back and neck are all Lou can see of him. His voice, which she has not heard for a while, seems new and strange, lower and rough. She thinks she will step upwards, stand beside him, in sight; but the man says again "No ladies in here." The long unbraced step is swaying beneath her. And in the cold wait while the man disappears (back through the house, his feet down the rear steps, crunch of snow in the yard) though she fixes on the firm back so recently familiar, she finds that it moves. Still as he is, merely facing the door, he is changing before her; sliding from the one she has gladly chosen through something newer—or older—toward what? Strangeness, surely. Can she bear this newness, require it like the old? She is no longer thinking of the perfect question; she must only make him speak—"I am freezing," *she says.*

*"You'll live," *he says. *He uses the new voice for her also but he does not turn.*

*"I was afraid of that," *she says.*

"Were afraid?"

"Still am."

His palm and the money are still extended— toward the bolted door. It is all he offers. He waits to give it.

And the man returns, two clear jars-full tucked under one arm. His other hand holds newspaper for wrapping.

*Todd says, *"I'll take it naked. No need to hide it. No law between here and where I'm headed."

*The man hands it over, naked glass as it is, and accepts the money; but before he even counts it, he studies Todd's face. (Lou studies the man to see what he finds.) Todd stands and bears the look; and at last the man says, *"Who put you on to me?"

*"A boy named Eborn—Todd Eborn," *he says—*his voice still stranger, as if bearded, veiled.*

*The man shakes his head. *"Not him," *he says. *"I have never heard of him."

"A boy about my size?—uglier, maybe?"

The man shakes his head.

Lou is burning to speak or to seize his full arms and turn him to see, but the one high step sways beneath her again. She is trapped, as on drifting ice.

"It was him," Todd says—or the boy there before her says. "He's a regular customer. Must come by night. Under cover of night."

The man says, "He might have tried—some few have but they found out I don't sell nothing *after dark. And never to drunks. I got rules to keep." He pauses, unfinished—"You remember I told you and you come again—"*

"I will," Todd says. "I'm glad to've found you."

"But leave your lady home."

"If she's mine, I will," Todd says and turns.

Lou has turned and gone, not hurried or in flight but unwelcome and puzzled, four steps in advance. She is now reluctant to see him though offered.

And he does not rush up to catch her but comes behind steadily, in all their old steps which are now a deep trough. He only says to her—still in sound of the house, the man in the door, his voice still altered— "You are with me, aren't you?"

Not turning back or slowing she nods once Yes. He takes that and they continue forward. Lou thinks she has risked loss again—or waste. This time it would be waste, caused by her own self, no question of luck. Her own need and readiness for ruin stand within her, full-grown, appalling. Death is not the only fear. Yet how can she face-round now, reclaim his face, say her love, await his answer?

They have come almost to the trees again, the end

of the clearing; Lou is passing the woodshed. Once hid in trees, the two of them hid, she will find her means to seize this hope. He is still behind her—that much is sure.

A voice, close-by, says "Boom!" once softly.

Lou falters an instant (is it he, changed again?— into what now and why and where will he stop; can he stop at all?). But the sound of his stride is steady behind so Lou goes on.

Then it comes again, louder—"Boom!," a girl's voice or the mockery of one.

Todd has stopped, is silent.

Lou takes the last step, unrushed, into woods; then from their bare shelter, stops, turns to see.

Todd is faced toward the woodshed—clearly himself again—but falling slowly, a feather in thick air, both hands (the jars pressed safe to his chest) clutch inward to his belly as though to stanch blood and his face is wrenched shut as though against pain. He drops to his knees, snow covers his thighs; his head rolls limp, eyes shut, on his chest.

"Lost," Lou thinks. "They all fly from me."

But of course then he smiles and looks up—not to Lou.

To a short dark girl in only a dress—a summer dress, loose-waisted, bare-armed—who holds with both arms against her shoulder a dead dry stick which she sights like a gun. She is also smiling and she says "I know you."

Todd nods to her, stands, puts a hushing finger to his open mouth, then waves once slightly and starts again.

Three steps toward Lou, his broad smile fading, before Lou can think shall she stand or run.

Then the girl drops her stick in the snow and says "When?"—to Todd's back only; he will not turn.

He moves on to Lou and does not stop till his free hand brushes her own, pale from fear. "Caught," he says.

She withdraws her hand, clenches it behind her but cannot withdraw her eyes from his face. "Everybody's caught," she says at last. Then she turns and walks ahead—a speed she chooses so that he can follow, whoever he is or will become.

It had taken Eborn three days to bring them to that, the leading and following, their hands crossed, their places swapped. The days had been stripped of all but the work, the effort to focus and hold a gaze which would be both recording and discovering and which, as it focused, would turn sight to fire, his vision the burning glass which makes fire from light (fire for what?— further seeing)—the work and a minimum of necessary fidgets, fumes of the fire (stops for coffee, the mail, long looks out windows, light meals, hasty signals to Jane). And when he had come to that, he stopped— tired and empty but also exuberant, sure that the scenes would extend before him and urgently needing to tell someone of his new hold on power, the circuit restored.

He telephoned Ted—it was just past five; Ted would surely be home. But the rings screwed on in a lonely vacuum; and Eborn's own headful of pleasure was draining—no chance of a refill today or tonight—when Ted came at last, winded from his yard (he'd been wrecking a chimney). Eborn thanked him for his poems, the one poem especially; he'd study them all but now—these three days—he'd been locked into new work of his own, work that had started with Ted's one poem on Lou Eborn's death. Or been forced by it, anyhow (its meager charm, its diminution of a sizable past—that he did not say).

Ted was puffing his gruff encouragement—saying, "When can I read it?"—when Jane walked in, home from work, normal time, went to Eborn where he hunched on the kitchen counter talking and ringed his thin bare wrist in greeting.

He smiled, told her "Ted"; then as she moved on to unload her groceries, he ended with Ted—"You can read it tomorrow if you'll promise not to speak, or give an opinion. I know it's good; it feels wide and clear; but I mustn't hear a word till I'm in head-deep—then rave away, I'll be past you and gone. But come by tonight after supper, why not, and I'll give you the carbon."

Ted had other plans but would see him soon, next day or two.

Eborn said "Right" and hung up smiling—but drained a little lower, all gift no receipt. So he looked to Jane, where she bent stuffing the icebox with radishes and celery, and began the sort of silence—the lodestone wait, unflickering look—that would calm her busyness, turn and draw her.

She turned at last, when her job was done; but she did not go to him, did not smile, and her stance was a wait not an offering.

"Tired?" he said.

She nodded, head stopping at the top of a nod, high, a little stretched, her chin catching late light that slatted cross the sink.

"I could take you out, save you cooking here—" He sprang to the floor from his seat on the counter, made a muffled clap with his hands—he was ready.

But she did not move.

He said again "Tired?" as though distracted, as though he had not already asked and been answered. His distraction was reverie, involuntary start of the process of transformation—this exhausted Jane (skin slightly thinner—more porous to light—her top lip slightly longer and drier) into what he had dreamt he needed, must shelter, seven years before. He had moved her backwards successfully in the instant it took her to gather and reply.

"I have told you Yes, Thomas. Tired from work—my deathless work—but dead-tired, bone-tired, from slouching out here, slinking round your stoop while you fling out the scraps to slick fat strangers."

He understood at once—he had phoned Ted not her, with his full good news—and though he coiled once at her Lazarine eloquence, he said only, "Jane, you had left the office; I couldn't phone the grocers—we are not kids at Christmas—and I had to thank Ted anyhow for his poem."

She stood her ground, sucked her cheek inward, gnawed.

"Understand?"

She nodded. "Understand is all I do. For once, Thomas—one day when I'm not looking—hit me hard in the chest with a mystery. Big as a boxcar and dirty brown. Let me *figure*, just once."

He nodded. "Forgiven?"

"—Never charged," she said. "Takes two to fail."

"Where shall we go?"

"For what?"

"Supper, Jane."

"Not tonight," she said. "Please eat what I cook. I wouldn't go out now, tired as this, to welcome Christ to the certified manger."

He agreed but did not offer to help and, though it was his impulse, did not move to touch her. Like his mother, she was hindered by kitchen help; and however forgiving, she gave off the odor of pure offense—*Do not stoop to touch me*—and would do so for hours, he knew.

So he waited—read till she called him in to eat, was silent at table till she offered talk.

His shirts were ruined by the laundry, weren't they?

They were but "No," he said, "not ruined exactly."

She was sorry; from now on she'd do them herself.

He looked up to test—was this the beginning of her amends?

She was busy cutting veal, her mouth still clamped. Not amends—she knew, as he did, she had not been wrong—but the habit and necessity of their lives, what she felt was their life: shirts can be well done; if others can't, I can.

He thanked her, was all.

But after they'd finished and she'd come from cleaning up and sat in her chair, he made his own beginning as obvious as paint, because it was his strong wish, seemed surely a need—"Will you listen to something?"

Of course she would.
"—But *only* listen?"
"Yes," she said.

He brought down the new twenty pages, still un-
typed—his quick script already, in the early pages only
three days old, sliding towards cipher; he must type
them tomorrow morning while he could—and sat to
read them to her. Had he done this before?—he spent a
moment wondering. Oh years ago when they both were
children, he'd have read her the poems he wrote for her
(baffling—baffled—and thickly crusted with exhausted
metaphor) and his first haunted stories (characters with
names like Laurance and Elaine who gave one another
cursed emeralds, and paid); but since he'd been serious
(accepted his life), he had read his own work aloud to
no one but himself-in-a-closet; and when he felt
tempted by a handsome invitation, he'd attend a campus reading by a visiting writer or buy a poet's record
and submit for three minutes to the warm bombard-
ment of narcissus petals. Now he must try again.

He started rapidly—title, opening formulae—then
looked to see her straining to chase his speed; then
slowed but struggled to clip back his wonder and pride
in each word, especially the ends of words (traps for
lingering, rest-stops, love-pits) and did not look up
again till he'd said the last sentence. Then he looked to
his watch not Jane—thirty minutes. Three days of
work—which focused the earnings of his thirty-odd
years on the sixteen and nineteen years of his young
parents—now thirty minutes. The quickness shocked

and frightened him. Too quick, surely, to inflict a wound or glow to a light.

He looked to Jane—reclined in her chair and facing him but closed still, glazed. He was forced to explain, to himself, to her—"That is not an end. There will be more scenes, all crucial ones which I didn't witness—some painful day in the midst of their courtship (which lasted six years), the day of their engagement, their honeymoon (they went to Florida on the Orange Blossom Special), then their early life together (one awful day in the late Depression, when Father was drinking out of control), the night I was started, the day of my birth. Well, you see what I'll have. It began with a poem Ted brought the other night, on Mother's death. Lovely but thin. Yet not—it made me see—as lean as what I'd granted her—"

Jane had not moved or mirrored his effort. She listened though.

He saw the chance and meant it; it was true— "What I'd granted *us*. It began with you—what you said that night when you'd read my piece on work. I had stripped Mother's life; your life—and ours. There were pure kinds of work that involved no products so were hardest of all, being fueled by nothing more visible than love. These scenes will be a chart of one kind, a work of love which will find exactly that—that love can be work."

She still had not moved.

So now he must force her undoubted gratitude. "Tell me what you think."

"Of what?"

"These pages."

"You said 'Only listen.' "

"Well, now I need an answer."

"Easy lies," she said. "—Your scene and everything you've said."

He was silent of course; he turned the pages, stared again at the last which was two-thirds empty, tried to read the end but could not see it—"I haven't finished."

"You will," she said. Still she had felt no need to move, even sit upright. If this was her uncollected force, what lay in reserve?

Nor had he looked up. If he did not confirm this by sight, it would fade; disarm itself—a letter not sent. Perhaps he had misheard, not understood. Or perhaps she had hared-off in anger and haste and would rise now to any calm chance at return. "If I can," he said. "This part *was* easy—the joy at the start, theirs and mine. The pain will come later, when they both strip-off. They've done that already though, haven't they?—seen their ugliest chances?"

She waited till he faced her. "You'll finish," she said.

What he saw was this—that her face, unchanged by their past seven years (only thinned and tightened), her face he had loved and needed and honored, had been all along (surely secret to both) witness, investigator, prosecutor; now judge and killer. What had she killed?—here was his triumph: nothing that had lived. Her recent great moment—for which seven years had only been training (surely secret to her?)—had been dirt on a corpse. Not even that; a corpse has moved, breathed a time or two, threaded its blood once at least through the careful net, retracted it once.

It was only eight-ten. He tested the prospect of four, five hours till the hope of sleep. He found himself calm, mind firm round its center (tomorrow, the work, scene two—*They Love*). He could do it, no question; that far, she was right. A houseless man, if he's seen roof and walls, can still build a house. Had better.

He stood. He would go for a drive—through town toward the country. The small box of blackness—only lights, from the panel and the odd shut house—would rest his eyes. His right eye was tugging, not badly but often.

Jane called him back. He was almost gone, nose already in the street, when she came to the top porch-step and waved. He knew now she would not offer remorse or justification; so he stopped, rolled his window down and waited.

She did not come down or raise her voice. Her natural voice carried—"Long-distance for you."

"Again?" he said, not knowing what he meant. "Who is it?"

"Personal," she said, "again."

He reversed the car three feet and left it.

Jane stayed in place on the top step, watching him.

He passed her silently—she waited behind—and went to the kitchen phone, walked not ran but seized already (the strings of his gut) against the threat to be flung again, whirled at the sick circumference of loss.

He was Thomas Eborn, yes.

But the operator said, "I apologize. I was holding for you and she let go. Busy as I am—"

"Who?" he said.

"I don't know her name, but I'll try to get her back."

A wait, sound of rustling paper, distant ring.

A woman's voice.

The operator said, "I have your party. Did you want him still?"

"Oh yes," the woman said. "I did not understand." She was winded and slow—"Tom?"

"Yes."

"It's Ida."

His only thought was, "There is nothing left to tell me; you know no one else." He said "Ida, are you well?"

"*I'm* well," she said, "but Tom, here I come wading in with trouble—"

He tried, as a kind of rescue, to see that—Ida, two hundred pounds, wading, waddling, in. Into what? "What?" he said.

"What time is it now?"

"Eight-twenty or so."

"Ten minutes ago then, I was out back with the dog, in the dark—it's not so dark—and he'd run down your way, your house; so I went on after him, down at the bottom by the gully, you know; and Tom, the door of your mother's house was open—the kitchen door—and a light was on. Were you over today?"

Was he? He could not think at first. "No, it's been three or four days and then I locked up."

"Well, I wanted to know."

That seemed all she needed. He rushed to stop her leaving—"Was anything stolen?"

"Oh I wouldn't know," she said. "I couldn't go in."

"Did you shut the door?"

"Oh I couldn't do that."

"Should I come?" he said.

"Who else?" she said.

Not another soul. The buck stopped here, though he thought for a moment he'd call Ted to join him—Ted had other plans. "I'll be there in half an hour," he said. "I had the car out." He remembered; three weeks ago, Ida to him—"Thank God, you knew." He was flinging, no question.

"I'll be here," she said.

"I'll stop by first."

When he got to the porch again, Jane was still there—or was there again. Seized though he was, he saw she had moved—she trailed a blue sweater she had not held before and she faced the car. He saw it, noted it, as fact not feeling, and felt no curiosity—or anger or pressure to give hurt for hurt. One war at a time—Jane had been bypassed; her possibly lethal charges postponed, wounds forbidden to bleed, by simple housebreakers. He stopped beside her. "I have got to go home. That was Ida Nolan. She's seen the house open, the kitchen light on. Someone's broken in." He went down a step. "I'll be back when I can."

Consciously or not, she had hid her sweater—wadded behind her, to give him free choice. "May I go?" she said.

"You're tired and I'll have to call the police—"

"I'm better," she said and found another lever—
"Tomorrow's Saturday. We could spend the night
there and I could work tomorrow till you had to come
back, packing things, cleaning."

"—If there's anything left." Another step. He
thought, at the rim of his mind, "I do not want or need
her tender amends"; but at core he was clung to all that
now mattered—the house had been breeched, maybe
final damage done to whatever he'd had, his last re-
serves of calm and weight—so he told her "Thank
you."

"Two minutes," she said. She rushed back in.

He went four steps farther, down and out to the
yard—clasped now in blackness by the low dense trees;
and to fill the wait, stave off other thoughts, he turned
to the house and watched the windows, counting as
accurately as he could the seconds Jane needed to pack
toothbrushes. But, helpless, he wondered as always on
leaving, could the house conceivably survive their absence?—the miles of hot wiring stay wrapped and safe,
all the pounds of oiled rag and airless paper not ex-
plode, the sewage not siphon, lightning not strike, pictures and books and odd money not be stolen? He had
managed to count through that—two hundred-
thirty—and now upstairs, their bedroom light vanished;
Jane had finished there. Less than four minutes; she
would need two more—lock the kitchen door, check
the windows, all the lights. Five, six minutes to shut-
down and go.

He could go now of course and save two minutes,
alone, stripped for speed. Could go for good, leave it all
forever, let her live on the fat he'd worked to pad round

them, her diet of lies. The mere thought cleaned him—he felt himself a bone sucked hollow and white, a mineral whistle. But the whole house was dark—sudden, sooner than he'd planned—and still for an instant.

He gathered to spring—but only in his head; feet stayed firm.

So she came out dark and down towards him, quite unreadably. He wanted a match or passing headlights to outline her now—show her need and purpose in leaping to this. But no car passed and he'd never smoked. Far as he could see, she came on steadily, by light of her own—he waited in place—but at him she faltered. Her blind body struck him and, in reflex, he grabbed; found her right hand, filled—her small college duffel stuffed with what, in five minutes, would hold them till morning. He pressed it harshly, canvas barely yielded. His mind inventoried—two pairs pajamas, two suits work-clothes, toothbrushes, toothpaste, razor, soap, comb; and cushioned in the heart, boxed and cherished through her haste, her love-equipment, the hopeful plumbing, her last dark ditch.

His eyes saw better as he turned to the car. He started and went forward silently. Then he heard her behind him. Her soft steps (in grass towards her side of the car) were blocked in his ears by a hate pure as coal.

FOUR

I<small>DA</small>'s house was empty. Her porch light burned but her car was gone and nothing answered Eborn's knock but the dog, in howling fury behind the door. He went to his own car, not meaning to speak (they had not said a hundred words on the trip; all his were answers).

But Jane said, "It's past nine o'clock. Where is she?"

"Off her head," he said and reversed the car, crept back toward his mother's, paused a moment in front—all the front windows dark—then moved forward down the steep drive to the back.

The kitchen door was open—wide, no reluctance—and the light was on. His headlights covered the path to the high stairs; he studied that—the grass seemed ranker, stronger by double, since he'd walked through on Wednesday to burn the papers. There were no signs of tracks, not from where he sat, no crushed footsteps or discarded loot.

Still separate, not looking to Jane, he moved—cut the lights, opened his door.

"Tom," she said.

He waited, turned away, one foot in damp weeds.

"You said the police. You should call them first, have them meet us here."

He sat another moment, then moved out entirely,

shut his door, went forward.

She rushed out also, spoke across the car—"You are playing the fool. It's dangerous, Tom."

He was on the first step. He stopped there and said, "Not *playing*. I *am*—fool, liar and coward. So they're all three going up these steps now, alone and bare, to face the Unknown."

She could not see his silent laugh but read it in his voice. "I'm coming," she said.

"You could use it," he said.

The house was empty—of people, at least. He had slowly established that minimal safety by working inward from the lighted kitchen (locking its door), through each dark room, each closet; Jane behind him, duffel in her hand—as what? weapon? charm? She had been his fear, not whoever might lunge from a corner at his throat. *Fear of what?*—he'd wondered as he sped through the search (that if she spoke again he'd turn and strike her? or order her out?).

He understood only when they'd checked the last room—his mother's, because it was naturally last, up-stairs-back—and Jane had sat on his mother's bed and smoothed with her free hand at dusty pleats in the cotton spread. The pleats were wrinkles left by his mother in her last few nights—the bed was unchanged. They seemed to him now, as he watched her in silence, the one thing left—one thing *she* had left him of all he'd had: that Jane was the breaker, the ravenous thief and, not appeased by all she'd ruined (their own careful truce, his work to preserve his parents' dignity, their small but firm beachheads in chaos), must even **now** press out wrinkles in cloth.

She was not facing him, did not understand.

He waited, in hope she would stop and stand; **but** at last, at the limit, he said "Are you frightened?"

"Not now. No more."

"Please go down then—I've locked the back door—and check for what's missing. I'll check up here."

"Will I know?"

"Know what?"

"What's missing."

"Just look. Help a little, please. You asked to come."

She nodded and went, left her duffel on the bed.

When he had heard her footsteps vanish into carpet downstairs, he went to the bed, took the duffel, leaned it against the wall, then tried with his palm, silently, to erase Jane's shape that lingered in the cloth; then sat and wept (first a sob too stifled to carry, then silent tears), accepting finally Jane's victory and, worse, its justice. There was only this—she had no real win: she had had no opponents. Not the ones she had seen at least, ranged hateful against her. Surely not his work. She had known, and without back-sliding or regret, the simple truth which had only knicked him in his brief sourest moments—that his work bore no likeness to what he'd intended for twelve years and had felt it achieving—an unhurried steady attention to mystery (whether threatening or buoying) which, for long-breathed spaces, did achieve its aim: *comprehension* (the facts and the answers) or, failing that, *celebration* at least, a seemly dance round the shrouded god or as firm a wall as a man could build to hold off madness, idleness, loss. An hour ago she'd showed it up in one phrase as infinitely less—a stove-in bladder, easy lies. Both *lies* and *easy* because each word had been founded-on and fed exclusively by the one thing his parents had thought they'd learned, what they'd offered him as their own life-earnings—the knowledge and ex- ample that love is possible, however scarce; that the aim of life, the end of human effort, is the comprehen- sion, loyalty, generosity which come at last (the light in the circle) to the few who can try—and what (despite his own cold heart) he'd peddled prettily till this after- noon, in all his work, his friendships, his marriage. His parents' try had at least been difficult; their lie a delu- sion never unmasked, whose remnants surrounded him—this back-broke house, helpless, wallowing in truckloads of dusty junk no ragman would buy; and it now raided and surely rifled.

He heard her walk to the foot of the stairs.

"Were the hedge-clippers here?"

He quickly stood, in case she should come—"The *what?*"

"—Electric clippers your father bought, with the

mile-long cord. Did you take them home?"

"No."

"They're gone then," she said. "I thought they were—empty box was lying on the tool-closet floor."

He did not answer, had barely heard, was in any case immune.

"What's missing up there?"

He quickly looked round him. *Missing!*—God, the room seemed stuffed, seemed pressurized to bursting with excess, wastage. Two of everything—and those two multiplying dizzily. He sat again softly on the edge of the bed. "Nothing yet," he said.

"Shall I call the police?"

The cold coil of fear. Caught at last—and rightly, his present offense being only the newest in a life-long chain with far-worse links that had passed unseen. No, he'd go along calmly. "I'll call," he said; then shook and grinned at his panicked dive.

"Check the jewelry?" she said.

He had not, and grinned deeper to think of it as jewelry. "No," he said and looked to the bureau, "but the box is here."

He went to the small brown leather box (heard Jane waiting for word downstairs), rubbed it with his thumbs (it was dry, needed oil) and opened on his mother's few pins and beads. The only two things of any value were there on top, untouched since he'd entertained—and quickly rejected—the thought of burying them with her, natural company. The pearls his father had given her at their marriage (cultured but good; even now, not yellowed) and the etched gold pin, quadrant of a circle, which had been her own mother's. Then a small knot of gold chains, odd earrings, the watch she'd abandoned unable to read. All there clearly, plus one thing he'd failed to notice last time, in the rush of the funeral—an inch of newsprint pinned to the top lining:

> *It is a pleasant thought that*
> *when you help a fellow up a steep hill,*
> *you get nearer to the top yourself.*

Pleasant thought. Easy. And dazed. And a lie. Top of what hill? Why climb it? What then?

Jane said "Tom, what's there?"

"Nothing," he said; then saw, in his head, himself as Cordelia—blond, white-gowned, soft heels dug-in to tell only truth which in fact will be lie, the white string hung from the cloud-blanked ceiling labeled *Pull Me*. You pull. A black anvil falls on your scrupulous head. *Nothing will come of nothing: speak again.* "Nothing gone, I mean. Not yet, up here." He heard Jane take the first two steps; she was coming, to help. "Keep looking down there," he said; he gabbled in the need to postpone facing her. "I'll call the police."

The phone in the upstairs hall worked, gladly.

And in less than five minutes (before he had checked all his mother's room), Jane called up, "Tom—" and the door-knocker slammed two times, a ram.

He went to the dark front room, looked out—a white cruise-car at the curb. Relief—they would actually come when you called (he had never called police before). Then an instant of fear—they had come too quickly, haste out of proportion to his mild complaint ("I think we may have had a small break-in"). How much faster for murder? a beating in progress? He saw (first time in three days) the dead boy, the chanting patrolman—"Tell me, tell *me*." And that was not finished. Even now, his name—as witness—was passing from cool hand to hand through unknown channels, eternally flourescent-lit.

Another two knocks. He'd never move.

But Jane called again, "Tom, you answer the door."

He thought, "She is worse-off than me; fears losing *me*" and clattered down the stairs to the locked front door.

The first one, he knew; remembered from school—Bo Browder, a boy two years his senior, a late-forties hood whom Eborn still saw clearly (though they'd never spoken) in duck's-ass hairdo, draped wine slacks, swagging keychain. Now the armed liveried Law. And a younger one behind him, short and cocked for all comers; both solemn as widows, unwilling to speak. Eborn said "Come in," backed towards the living room; and they came a few feet, then stopped as if at the stink of ambush.

"You're Evern?" Browder said.

He heard it as "Even," looked to Jane for response—confirmation, denial.

She said "Eborn, Thomas Eborn" and pointed to Tom.

Browder smiled back, sour, to his mate as if to say, "Cat's got his tongue. Let's deal with her"; then motioned Jane downward—"All right. Take a seat. We'll ask a few questions."

Jane sat in the large brown corner arm-chair and Eborn—to his own amazement—on its stool, thinking only "They wear their hats indoors."

Browder stood in the center, his mate near the door—still covering an exit! "This your home?" he said. He was speaking to Jane.

"His," she said. "My husband's."

"—My parents'." Eborn took his chance. "I live in Fenton, my wife and I. My mother lived here till her death last month. I teach, so the house has been locked since then till I had free time to come over, close it down, put it up for sale. But I was here three days ago, sorting papers. It was all safe then. I locked up tightly —though there's been no trouble on this street for years; can't *remember* trouble—"

"Why are you here now then?" Browder said.

His young mate nodded.

Eborn could not think.

"—Meaning what?" Jane said. "It's ours to use."

Browder said, "Right, lady. What I meant was, who told you the house had been entered?"

Eborn said, "A neighbor. Mrs. Ida Nolan, my mother's best friend, lives two houses down, a widow with a dog. She phoned me an hour ago in Fenton. She'd been walking her dog down back of the lot and saw a light on in the kitchen up here and the back door open. We came at once."

"Where is she?" Browder said.

Eborn craned to see out the window, Ida's way. He felt he must bury his own puzzlement to shelter Ida. "Not at home," he said.

"Wonder why not?"—the younger's first word.

Browder nodded. "I wonder. Most widows with dogs are home by nine, locked in for the night. Where you think she's gone?"

"No idea," Eborn said.

"We'll need to see her."

"I doubt it," Eborn said. "I've told you what she knows. She didn't come in, hasn't been in once since my mother's funeral. She saw the light on, the door standing open and called me—that's all."

"You don't want to see her yourself, about this?—ask her anything?"

"Not a thing," Eborn said at once. "I'm sorry I bothered you to come out tonight. There are worse things happening."

"Not many," Browder said. "—Your mother's place broke by strangers at night. Your place now."

"Mine and the bank's—till I clear out and sell it." He saw he'd shocked Browder.

"You sound glad about it—your robbery here." Browder looked round the room. "But they didn't help you much with the clearing out, did they?"

"That's it," Eborn said, "—why I'm sorry I called, called yet anyhow. Nothing seems missing."

"You've looked all around?"

"You came so fast, no. My wife's looked down here and I was looking upstairs—"

"And nothing's gone?—no money, jewelry, silver?"

"The hedge-clippers," Jane said. "Electric hedge-clippers."

Browder said "Where were they?"

"In the kitchen tool-closet. I found the empty box on the floor."

"Did you have a yard man?"

Eborn said, "Same one for twenty years."

"When was he here last?"

"The day of the funeral."

"Did he use those clippers?"

"Did he, Jane? I was busy."

"Oh yes. Nothing else. He's proud of those." She heard her own error, an instant late.

"Did he have a house key?"

Jane said "Did he, Tom?"

"Never. No."

Browder said "What's his name?"

Eborn stood. "Look, I've filed no formal complaint. Let's drop it all."

Browder paused a moment, looked round again; his mate watched him closely. "You have theft insurance at least, I guess?—that much protection?"

"Yes."

"You need us then. No other way."

Eborn said "No way for what?"

"To get your new clippers"—Browder's mate again, smiling.

"And close down your family home with respect"—Browder, graver than ever. "You want that, don't you?" Straight at Eborn, no blinking.

Eborn stared back in silence.

So Browder tried at Jane—"You want that, don't you?"

Eborn looked back to her. Let her say. She had won it.

She nodded Yes to Browder, said to Eborn "He's right."

Browder'd turned already. "Where's the door they broke?"

Eborn did not rise, so when silence was intolerable, Jane stood and said "The kitchen—back here," and led off that way but turned after four steps and looked through the champing policemen to Eborn.

He sat on the stool and looked to a table against the far wall, a picture propped there in a cheap easel frame—his mother five years ago at Christmas, her large head tipped back, bright eyes on the flashbulb, mouth wide to laugh or to launch a small joke like a fresh-painted dinghy any moment now, to sweeten the day.

And Jane, standing, caught across her mouth again the warm wash of Mrs. Eborn's laughter, a corrosive; clamped her teeth at the pain. But Thomas was still, more than still—*stopped*, she saw. The blanched paralysis of one frame frozen in a moving film—no hope of start, continued action, or this moment used for future gestures, promises fulfilled or worked-at at least.

It had lasted an instant—so short the police had never broke step—but she knew at the end something vital had died, the ultimate fuel of their life was used: her own curiosity, her need to know him. He was known. Harmless, tolerable, requiring close care—could she give it? She did not know, not yet.

Nor did she know what he thought, locked there; he'd remembered his mother's ungiven message and searched her laughing face for it, now.

Jane turned again, kept her lead on the men; and Eborn followed at a little distance.

*   *   *

The kitchen door had been entered neatly, no forcing; a passkey maybe. Browder rattled the handles awhile, rapped the pane; then asked, "How many have keys to this door?"

Jane said "Only him" (not knowing of Ida's) and flicked toward Eborn.

Browder had accepted her answer, gone on, when Eborn stepped up a little and said "Only me."

Browder locked the door again and turned his back to it—he was studying the room.

Jane said "Fingerprints?"

The younger answered. "Too late. No use. He's rubbed all over it." He nodded toward Eborn.

"I have," Eborn said.

"I knew," Browder said. He turned to his mate. "Jimmy, take him upstairs. Help him finish his search, and check all windows to see they're locked. Me and her'll look down here."

So Eborn climbed behind Jimmy slowly; and at the top—when Jimmy turned right toward his mother's room—Eborn said only, "Left. I have checked the right." Jimmy accepted and went left—delicately! the balls of his feet—and Eborn spoke again only when questioned (Jimmy's attempts to do his job and also ease the pain)—

"Have any radios or record-players round?"

"A radio. It's here."

"Any electric razors?—since he seemed to like cutting."

"No. My mother didn't shave."

"That your grandmother there? I'd've known her anywhere." (It was Stuart's George Washington, framed, in a bedroom.)

Eborn nodded—"Yes, it favors"—and smiled. Then he turned toward the steps. "That's all. He didn't come up, apparently."

Jimmy said, "Maybe not but let me check the rest. You may have missed something—the window maybe."

Eborn could not refuse. The *rest* was his mother's. He knew he should feel protective toward it—her bed safe from strangers. But he did not. He led the way, opened the door, stood aside on the sill for Jimmy.

Jimmy stopped by the bed, stood perfectly still (the first time yet; a nervous boy), then looked from left to right very slowly, his neck turning through a constricted arc as though bound by a crick, his look finally stopping on the bedside table—the snapshots there, the crucifix above.

Eborn waited behind him, mildly wondering where the boy thought he was, what he'd ask when he turned any moment now.

He did not turn but reached up quickly and removed his hat, held it awkwardly, crotch-level in both twitching hands.

Eborn forced down a smile and took a step forward, toward the window to check.

Browder said, from the foot of the steps, "Mr. Evern?"

Eborn stopped in place—"Yes?"

"Step down here please."

Eborn listened intensely. The house was silent. He knew that he listened for news of Jane—what had she done? found? what face would she bear? was she there at all? No hint.

Jimmy watched him.

Browder said "Jimmy too."

Eborn stood back for Jimmy to lead the way, but Jimmy put his hat on and waved Eborn forward.

Browder stood at the foot of the stairs, in the kitchen, looking toward Jane.

Jane stood at the far wall, five yards away, one hand on the stove, looking down at it.

Eborn thought, "She is cooking them something—but what?" The house was empty; and when he looked, the top of the stove was clear of pans. He looked back to Jimmy who stood higher now, still on the last step; but Jane faced Browder. Eborn asked Browder, "What?"

Browder asked Jimmy—"Anything else gone?"

"Nothing, and all the windows were locked."

"Nothing else here either, just the hedge-clippers." Then he looked to Eborn. "But they did leave a sign—I'm sorry to tell you. Nothing so rare in cases like this—"

"What?" Eborn said.

"In the breakfast room," he said, "—far corner, by the window."

Jane nodded when he looked to her from that distance; but when he went forward, nearly brushing her arm, she looked down again and did not move.

If they'd had the light on there, they'd turned it off so the alcove was dim and the far corner dark, shaded by the breakfast table (still in its green cloth, grainy with crumbs, splotched with the coffee his mother blindly sloshed). No one had followed. He stood in the corner the instant it took his eyes to adjust, then bent a little. The smell was dead—no smell at all—so his first thought was "A plastic joke, quite realistic."

Steps behind him. Browder said, at his back—too close, too close—"Mr. Evern, I can't speak for other towns; but this place is full of men—men *and* women—commoner than hogs."

Eborn bent nearer to it. A real turd then. "Personal!" he thought first—dry and tightly coiled. Neat and absurdly concealed, a dark corner. Why not bold in the center of the kitchen, smeared about and bathed in light? Why not in the sink? Or if not intended as stinking affront, why not ten yards away in the downstairs toilet? "A failure of nerve," he thought; saw the poor man—boy?—hunkered here straining, then rising cramped, his own bung filthy as the floor.

More steps. Jimmy now, craning to see. Face blushed at the sight. "That happens, Mr. Evern. Damnedest town on earth."

Eborn said, "I always liked it here"; but thought, "Of course it's the last of last straws, a high-school notion of the symbol for *finished*—signed and sealed." Still facing it, he waited for the weight to fall—tears, laughter, rage. Nothing fell, or rose. No one moved again. No sounds of breath. So he looked back to Jane, through Browder and Jimmy, in hopes of a sign from her at least—regret, tears even, or the taut flush of triumph.

There they were—steady tears, which she knuckled

away. Their single chance, single guarantee, of contin-
uation.

He looked to Browder. "Bo, are you done?" His
voice was firm but softer than he meant, and Browder's
old hood-name had slipped through his teeth.

Browder heard the tone, took his nickname as
natural (though his nameplate said *Robert*), glanced
back to Jimmy, then said, "—For tonight. We'll leave
you now. Will you just do this?—telephone me tomorrow and I'll come out or you come down and sign the
report?"

All this treacherous tenderness, gaseous food.
Eborn said, "I will, in the morning. Thanks" and
stepped through to lead them out the front. They
touched their hats to Jane and followed him.

Eborn watched from the porch till they vanished
entirely, their taillights snuffed by trees at the corner.
He even told himself, "They are busy men, already by
now they've been called elsewhere, they will not come
back." Then he went in, locked the front door behind
him, switched off the porch light and went to the
kitchen.

Jane was in the alcove, splashing the pile with
disinfectant.

He knew she'd heard his steps, could hear his near
breathing; but she did not look, made no use of her
face, relied on the force of her neck and back—the
martyr's hunched acceptance. Again he waited for the
crush of *something*—revulsion or tenderness. Again
nothing fell. He saw that her left hand held paper

towels and then she stooped. "Come out," he said, more tired than rough.

She stood and turned, white and papery from the effort. "No, Tom," she said, "go and do something else—sit down, sort books."

"That's mine to do. You sort those dishes"—he thumbed towards the cupboards.

She only turned back and crouched again quickly.

He took the three steps, then paused above her, then bent to touch her shoulder—"Thank you but No." He touched her neck. "Thank you—"

She stopped, stood—he gave her room—and left the corner, leaving towels and spray behind on the floor.

He checked her profile and back for anger. She went too quickly so he said again "Thank you."

She did not reply.

He watched her scrub her hands at the sink and dry them slowly. Then when choices lay open to her— turn on him hurtfully, go for good—she stepped to the cupboard, opened, studied a moment, then took down dishes as he'd asked her to do.

He had not even gagged and, as he washed in the downstairs toilet, he saw himself smiling in the scabby mirror and thought "There is progress," remembering the time not two years ago when he'd had to leave a student party he and Jane were chaperoning after Norman Gaul, a drunk halfback, had spat in the punchbowl. He was calm now—tired of course (a far rougher day than the crapper had had), a little numb maybe but far from sleepy. He'd go up and sort the books at last.

Someone tried the front door. He heard the loud click and a shoulder heaved against it. He stood, hands in towel.

Jane's dishes stopped, waited. Four or five seconds' silence. Then the door-knocker, twice. More silence.

Jane said "Tom?"

Nine-thirty. Who and why? "—I'll go." He went quickly.

It was Ida, bare-armed (upper arms like loaves set to rise against her breasts) and puffing from the hundred-yard walk, hands full. "Did you miss me?" she said.

He towed her up the last step. "I always miss you."

"No, just now, I mean—when you first came over."

"I tried your door, yes."

"Well, I thought I could help best by laying-in some breakfast food—you'll spend the night, won't you?"

"Here—yes."

"I knew you would, since you haven't been lately; and I knew there was nothing down here to eat so I went to the night-market—eggs and bacon." She weighed them out on her small hands before her. "—And a jar of coffee" (buried under one arm).

"You're so right," he said.

"I do what I can—know my limits, that's all." She still wheezed—the Little-Engine-That-Could. "Jane come with you?"

"Yes."

"I knew she would, since she has tomorrow off and

hasn't been over since the funeral, has she?"

He listened for Jane in the kitchen.

Silence. Lurked among dozens of cracked jelly-glasses, awaiting insult.

"I was here," he said, "—this past Wednesday, I guess, but had to rush home; so I didn't get to see you."

Ida touched his arm, glanced toward the hidden kitchen, dropped her voice—"Don't let me down." Her eyes widened on him and were full—tears? rheum?

He could not tell which and did not understand her. How let her down? He had not spent an hour with Ida Nolan in the past ten years. But he said "I'll try," forced himself to touch her hand (a hot little plush unused pincushion). Then to break the spell he said "Jane's back here," though he'd hoped to keep Ida out of the kitchen, the breakfast room still strong with Lysol.

She toddled behind him and said at once, "Scrubbing floors at midnight, Jane?—beyond the call of duty; still, it's stars in your crown."

"Tom's crown," Jane said, looking up unsmiling.

Eborn mugged a silent No to Jane behind Ida's back.

Jane worked on, sorting.

"Straightening cupboards?" Ida said. She had opened the refrigerator, loaded in her gifts.

"—Weeding," Jane said, "thirty years of glasses."

"You're not renting furnished?" Ida said to Eborn.

"Not renting at all, no."

Ida stood in place a moment looking round, as on a tour; then said "Who's for coffee?"—producing her jar.

Jane did not look.

Eborn said "All right" and reached for the jar.

"Let me," Ida said. "I've made it here hundreds of times for your Mom."

Eborn dangled idle in the midst of the room as Ida warmed water, found three mugs, spoons and sugar. Jane had still not looked again, only edged away from Ida at the stove; so his thought was to move them all out of here to the living room—a quick calm coffee, then Ida home to bed. Jane had taken down a tray. He reached for that—to load on the coffee, lead them out of here.

Jane said "Not for me."

"Why?" Ida said.

"I'd never sleep."

"That's a superstition," Ida said. "Soothes you off."

"I'm loyal to my superstitions," Jane said. "Sorry."

Eborn held out the tray toward Ida, ready. "You and I then, Ida—realists both. In the living room, nice easy chairs."

But Ida moved off toward the breakfast room, the mugs in hand. "Living room? I'm nobody's parlor company, God knows. Sit here. I wouldn't know how to swallow up-front." She sat at the table, opposite the scrubbed corner; set Eborn's mug at the head, on her left. "We'll sit here and keep Jane company while she works."

He could only sit—and thank God she hadn't cooked up any eggs. He studied his coffee but felt Ida's eyes on him.

"What had happened?" she said at last, voice lowered and tenderized.

He faced her, baffled.

"—When you got here tonight?—the back door, the light."

"Nothing very much. We've searched through the house."

"Nothing missing," she said—statement not question.

"One thing—the hedge-clippers."

"Oh those," she said—she smiled, nodded knowingly—"I've got those. Nathan left them with me the day of the funeral. He came on to my yard once he'd done yours, and he brought your clippers as he always does (mine are pre-Stone Age); but before he was through, your crowd was gathering thick down here so I told him just to leave them in my shed—I'd speak to you."

That had turned Jane round—with a stare for Ida so fixed and grave that Ida answered.

She said to Jane, "Do you need them tonight? I'll go for them now." But her tone was high, exhilarant not cowed.

Eborn said "Don't be silly."

Jane said, "Of course not. I'm just relieved."

Ida set down her mug, spread the cloth out round it with the palms of her hands, let the silence continue—Jane back to her work, Eborn looking vaguely down—then she said "I'm not."

Eborn said "Not what?"

"Not relieved. I *knew*."

Jane turned again. "Knew what?"

"—That nothing was gone, that you'd find it all

here." She was speaking to Tom—to his eyes, unblinking—no notice of Jane.

Eborn held her stare and thought, "She's off, cracked as any bell"; but before he could plan a new peaceful tack, she switched to Jane.

"Jane, sit here please and hear me now. I know a few things, however dumb I look; and they're for both of you."

Jane yielded, came and sat on Ida's right, directly facing Tom. "All right," she said.

Ida said, "Now hear me all the way before you start talking. This is not a short story. You could tell it better, Tom—really beautifully—but it's God's plain truth. I'm the one alive that knows it, so it looks like it's me that's been picked out to tell you. You may not believe me—I tried to escape it. You want to know where I was just now, when I wasn't at home?" She had not been rhetorical; she waited for Eborn's permission to proceed.

"Gone for our breakfast food, you said."

"I said it—and I lied. I've had those groceries for days—oh they're fresh!" (to Jane, smiling)—"and I haven't been out after dark for years. But I went tonight, when I'd hung-up on you. *Ran*." Another wait.

Eborn searched her face for coyness (her need to make him beg) but found pained reluctance. He said "Why, Ida?"

"I couldn't face coming in here," she said.

"It was a bit scarey."

"Not that, not that. *I* live alone, shuffle round my pitch-black house all night, the nights I don't sleep—most nights now. What wants to hurt me? Oh cancer may have started in me just this minute or a throw-rug could slip from beneath me tomorrow and I crush my hip—I can't stop those. And I can't stop my duty to you two either, though I tried to run. I didn't think I had the strength to watch you find them—"

"There was no one here," Eborn said.

Ida smiled, to no one—the black window opposite—then took her first swallow of coffee loudly, then changed her tack. Her whole trunk showed it, settled a little, arms puddled on the table. "You said you weren't renting. Are you moving over then?—you two over here?"

Jane shook her head but the question was to Tom. He said, "No, Ida. We work in Fenton so we need to live there."

"Just twenty-five miles," she said. "Thirty, at most."

"It's too far, Ida."

"When they have good homes, people drive hours—gladly—to get to work."

"We have a home, Ida—five minutes from work. Come and see us when you're lonely."

Jane nodded to second the invitation.

Ida nodded also, rapidly and flushing. "I'm not speaking of *me* and I'm not begging company— understand that much before I go on." She waited.

"Right," Eborn said.

"I'm speaking of you two." She looked up to Jane—" 'With what right?' you're asking. And I've asked myself this whole evening long, since I saw that door open, that light burning. The answer is I *do* have the right, the duty—and it's from the dead, put on me by the dead."

Eborn looked to Jane, who bore Ida's stare. He checked his watch—only nine forty-five. He could not plead bedtime and send her home; yet Jane seemed sealed in a motionless flinch—or, worse, reeling tightly to snap and flail. He touched Ida's arm—"Speak of us then please."

"You don't have a good home. I know that much. I see it with my own eyes—seven years, no children, both of you thin as slats—and your Mom told me too." She had turned again to Jane.

"His mother," Jane said.

"His mother, right—but she loved you too and worried her heart out these last few years."

"I don't doubt she worried," Jane said, "but not loved."

Eborn frowned but was silent.

"Fair enough," Ida said. "What mother ever did? But she cared, and for both—cared that, once she was gone, you would make a life—"

Jane said "You mean a child?"

"Not necessarily. No, not at all. I'm a good black Catholic but people come in pairs not threes or fives—I know that now. And your mother knew it, Tom— had it ground in her teeth once Todd had died and you'd moved out."

"People *do* that, Ida," Eborn said, "—move out, grow up, alter their lives."

"And good luck," Ida said, quick and hot. Her vehemence shocked her. Again she paused to drink.

Jane moved to stand, return to work.

Ida said "Wait," all but whispering.

Jane said, "It's late. There's so much to do."

"Give me three more minutes," Ida said. "Then I'll go."

Jane nodded, sat back.

Ida said, "You're meaning to sell this house?" She struck the table at right angles with a finger as though the table alone were the house.

Eborn said "Yes."

"Because it's a nuisance, excess baggage?"

"All right—put it that way."

"But do you know who was in here tonight?"

"No, Ida, I don't."

"Housebreakers, you think—don't you?"

"Yes," he said (not saying he knew).

"No," she said, "—the owners."

"That's me," he said, "—us, Jane and I."

"It's your Mom and Dad," she said. "They were here."

Jane stood, not speaking, and went to the cupboard; quietly started her work again.

Ida took no notice. This, now, was for Thomas. "I know you must think I have lost my mind—I live alone and watch a lot of TV, I grant—and Catholics are spooky. But I'm telling the pure truth—your Mom and Dad were here. Are still here, Tom." She still struck down at the table, one finger.

He had a quick sight, in his head, of his parents (he'd never said "Mom" and "Dad" in his life) as middle-aged ghosts, thick-waisted, unsteady in bifocal glasses, lurching through this forty-year-old sagging house with nothing to haunt but stacks of *Reader's Digests*, moth-tunneled carpets, a cracked TV, their marriage bed (still crusted beneath its quilted pad with the dried wet dreams, concentric and copious, of his mother's college-roomers)—Heathcliff and Cathy wheezing and varicose, hemorrhoidal, dry; dead too late!

"Ida," he said, "they were not here tonight, wherever they are. But this house was entered. You've got the clippers so nothing was stolen; but something was left—in plain shanty-Irish, a coil of shit on this breakfast room floor. As human as that. End of story. Sorry." He stood in place—ten o'clock; he was tired.

Jane turned to face him—also exhausted, able for nothing more harmful than sleep.

But Ida sat still, was shaking her head—though downward at her cup.

Eborn feared tears from her, the false extrication they would require.

When she looked up, her slack face was drawn, smoothed in a smile. "Not ended at all. That's nothing," she said. "Just coincidence—a bad boy or two, that needs a good smack. Not ended, Tom. Your Mom and Dad *win*. There's another story—or there's more to yours."

"You said three minutes, Ida, a long time ago."

"*You* broke in," she said. "My time's not up—and thank God for it. You'll thank God for it. You've forced my hand so I know she'll forgive me. I'll tell you her secret."

Eborn did not sit but he waited and listened.

"The day of her death, she spent with me—you remember that. Every morning for years. She'd come up oh by ten; and we'd watch a few game-shows, then fix our lunch—she'd bring little jars of this and that, though I always had far more than we needed! Once she went on a cottage-cheese diet for ten days or so and gained four pounds! It really upset her—hacked her, you know—but she stuck it out another day or two, till one day I looked at her carton of cheese. It was whole-milk cheese—cream and all! She'd been buying it blind, God love her heart. Said the package was prettier—brighter, she meant. But that last morning she came a little late, and empty-handed. I was already parked by the TV of course; so when I heard her knock, I just yelled her in—didn't go to meet her. She came and sat across from me on the sofa and we didn't say more than Boo till it ended—our precious program—but I could see, from the side of my eye, there was something wrong, changed at least, *new*. Not her clothes or looks, more the air around her. When the show was over, I turned down the volume and waited for her news— she'd always have something, if only the latest word on her weight; and I'd tell her mine (both whispering the figures) and we'd moan a minute or two before lunch. But she passed up the chance that morning, just sat; so I dusted my flowers—something DuPont; florlon?—and watched her in the mirror. She was inside-out. —Oh see what I mean: she had dived off into herself, for some-thing. She wasn't that inward a person—was she?—so I thought she was sick and, me and my mouth, I said, 'Lou, what's wrong? You're blue today.' She smiled, came out a bit—about two inches!—and said, 'Not *wrong*, not *blue* at all—*hung-over*, I guess.' —'Hung-over?' I said—I must have yelled. I mean, we'd drink a glass of sherry now and then or a beer with our lunch some hot summer days; but Lou? hung-over at noon on a week-day? I think I was shocked and I must have

showed it. —'Worse than that,' she said; then 'Ida, I
don't know what to call it.' —'Say *something*,' I said;
that's been my creed. So she said, 'Whatever it is, it's a
secret.' I nodded to that and she said, 'Well, you know
how, every night, I take off my clothes about half-past-
eleven and put on pajamas and lie on the couch in the
den and watch TV, always Johnny Carson—and always
doze off, silly fool, lying there and wake up at two or
three a.m. with the empty tube there blasting beside
me. Last night I did all that—and went to sleep and
woke up at two, with the set still jittering. I sat upright
on the couch and shook my head and said—
aloud—"Me and my foolish naps" and saw Todd sitting in his chair on my right. Three feet away, as
natural as you, not speaking and looking towards the
door. It was any night of my life, I must have thought;
so I stood up and went to the TV, switched it off and
walked through the living room, dining room, to the
downstairs bath and was there, on the seat, thinking
"Todd needs a haircut" before I knew what had happened, was happening. Twelve years. I was not
afraid—that's the other sure thing; the first is, Todd
was there where he hadn't been for twelve years—I
didn't even think of being afraid. I was still as calm as
any night, calmer. I got up. I took my time and walked
back carefully towards the den and stopped in the door.
By then, the chair was empty.' —Well, Tom, I didn't
know a word to say—what could I do? genuflect? bless
myself? All I could think was, 'This girl is not
lying—and was not dreaming.' She never lied to me in
all those years—and I'd told her things that would curl
a crook's hair. Tom, I thought, like her, it was any
other day so I said 'Lunch-time.' Imagine that. Then as

we headed in to the kitchen to fix it, I did, thank God, have the sense to say, 'It's a message from God, Lou.' —'I know that,' she said. She was dead in half-an-hour—or taken, her vein burst, she pressing her forehead as if, sweet girl, she could fight that warning, refuse that call."

Sandbagged, he sat, knowing only this—he did not doubt for an instant Ida's truthfulness or, deeper beyond, his mother's truth; the truth of her memory as of her vision, her corporal summons from a standard night to the sill of death. He only wondered, "Was he young or old—my father, for her? Did she see the boy she first loved and married or the man who died?" He tried to ask Ida now, looked up to her.

She, in tears of course, was facing him; touched him once—his pounding wrist; said before he could speak, "They are here, Tom, and you can't take it from them."

He looked.

They were. Beyond him and Ida their blurring messenger, between him and Jane's still busy back, they occupied space as firmly as the stove, though in the bright room, they stood in murk like a skin around them—grime or stain, which shielded them in their starved humiliation from his clear sight, his pity, his new rush of guilt. His first thought was that he must not stare—he would deepen their shame, would signal their presence to Ida and Jane—but they looked to him, he could see that much; pressed through the muffle of air toward him. "It was not a secret," he thought, "not for Ida. They meant it for me, their message for me, delivered at last." —What he'd already known—the hungry dead—and worked to help. So his work, his *knowledge,* was true not lies. That at least could continue. He could not keep off a smile. It spread.

By then, in the silence, Jane and Ida had looked—what was on his face? They moved with help toward him.

But he waved them back, his hand a slow oar in hot thick air. The room was filling, being filled, in strokes. Again. He remembered the day of her death, his nap, the pressed room. Filling with what?

Light. Theirs. There, pumping from them like arterial blood till they showed quite clearly, in their perfect youth, years before his birth. He still smiled—to be their one product, their hope, the agent now of their rehabilitation.

But they did not smile. Nor look at him. They do not move! He sees that, always, from the first, they have faced one another only, static in ecstasy, sealed in their needlessness, one another's goal—won at last and for good. Oh won at the start—gift not reward. Only *light* moves—their effortless product, only product; bilges around him, his eyes, cracked lips. He must shut against it. His eyes, lips refuse—even ears; it is audible, the roar of light. He knows he must stand in it all his life—and, worse, beyond—in full sight of them, their atrocious joy; but separate, lidless, scalding in their trail. He thinks that he speaks the worst he knows, means to say aloud to the bursting room, "The dead have their own lives."

The room, though, is still. No one has breathed.

REYNOLDS PRICE

Born in Macon, North Carolina in 1933, Reynolds Price attended small North Carolina schools and received his Bachelor of Arts degree from Duke University. As a Rhodes Scholar he studied for three years at Merton College, Oxford, receiving the Bachelor of Letters. In 1958 he returned to Duke where he teaches in the Department of English. There he began and completed *A Long and Happy Life* which was published in 1962 and received the award of the William Faulkner Foundation for a notable first novel. In the summer of 1961 he again traveled to England where he worked for a year at the stories which were published in 1963 as *The Names and Faces of Heroes*. 1966 saw the publication of his novel *A Generous Man*.